by John Yau

POETRY AND PROSE

Crossing Canal Street (1976)
The Reading of an Ever-Changing Tale (1977)
Sometimes (1979)
The Sleepless Night of Eugene Delacroix (1980)
Notarikon (1981)
    (with drawings by Jake Berthot)
Broken Off by the Music (1981)
Corpse and Mirror (1983)
Dragon's Blood (1989)
    (with drawings by Toni Grand)
Radiant Silhouette:New & Selected Work 1974–1988 (1989)
Big City Primer: Reading New York at the End of the Twentieth
    Century (1991)
    (photographs by Bill Barrette)
Giant Wall (1991)
    (with etchings by Jürgen Partenheimer)
Flee Advice (1991)
    (with drawings by Suzanne McClelland)
Edificio Sayonara (1992)
Postcards from Trakl (1994)
    (with etchings by Bill Jensen)
Hawaiian Cowboys (1995)
Genghis Chan: Private Eye (forthcoming)
    (with lithographs by Ed Paschke)

MONOGRAPHS

Forrest Bess (1988)
Brice Marden: A Vision of the Unsayable (1988)
Don Van Vliet (1991)
Miguel Angel Rios (1991)
A. R. Penck (1993)
In the Realm of Appearances: The Art of Andy Warhol (1993)

EDITOR

The Collected Poems of Fairfield Porter (1985)
    (with David Kermani)

JOHN YAU
HAWAIIAN COWBOYS

BLACK SPARROW PRESS
SANTA ROSA
1995

ACKNOWLEDGMENTS

Some of these stories appeared in a slightly different form in the following publications: "Sand" in *Lacanian Ink,* "A New Set of Rules Every Other Day" in *VLS,* "A New Beginning" in *First Intensity,* "The Language of Love" in *Public* (Canada), "The Things You Said to Me When We Were Lost" in *ZYZZYVA,* "Clothes Make the Man" in *Provincetown Arts,* "Family Album" (under the title "Photographs for an Album [Third Version]") in *Charlie Chan Is Dead: An Anthology of Contemporary Asian American Fiction* (Penguin Books, 1993), Edited and with an Introduction by Jessica Hagedorn and a Preface by Elaine Kim.

Second Printing

Black Sparrow Press books are printed on acid-free paper.

LIBRARY OF CONGRESS CATALOGING-IN-PUBLICATION DATA

Yau, John, 1950-
  Hawaiian cowboys / John Yau.
    p.   cm.
    ISBN 0-87685-956-2 (pbk.). — ISBN 0-87685-957-0 (cloth trade). — ISBN 0-87685-958-9 (signed cloth)
    1. Manhattan (New York, N.Y.)—Social life and customs—Fiction. 2. Alienation (Social psychology)—Fiction. 3. Social isolation—Fiction. I. Title.
PS3575.A9H39   1995
813'.54—dc20   94-39213
                                                        CIP

For Burt Held
who lives
in Waitakere, N.Z.

Table of Contents

HAWAIIAN COWBOYS

The Woman Across the Hall

I'm one of those people who never put a gravestone above his parents, who are lying at the bottom of an incline in a suburban cemetery. My mother died first, a few months before my father. As the limousine brought us through the cemetery, I noticed a black basalt gravestone with neat, vertical rows of Chinese ideograms. My father saw it at the same time. "She would never want Chinese on her gravestone. Never. She had become an American by the time she died."

I wanted to remind my father that they never stopped speaking Chinese to each other and they never started speaking it to me, but it was too late. The next time I rode in a limousine through the cemetery I saw the stone again, the gold ideograms like skinny incisions in the polished black surface. I couldn't read it and I still didn't know what, if anything, I would put on a stone erected at the head of my parents' graves, two memories lying side by side. Could I use "beloved" when I didn't love them and hardly knew them?

There are certain memories that pick at you, as if you are a scab trying to cover a small but persistent wound.

Whenever I happen to cross Canal Street and find myself threading my way through the throngs of old people leaving Chinatown, a little bit annoyed by it all, I remember my first apartment and the old woman who lived across the hall. This happened twenty-five years ago in Allston, which is, as far as I am concerned, really an ugly appendage of Boston. There were no magnificent museums, no venerable, old concert halls, no tall or stately government buildings, and no train stations in Allston, just anonymous neighborhoods sliding quietly into oblivion.

By the end of my freshman year I was tired of having a roommate, as well as living in a new highrise dormitory, and, before classes started that fall, I managed to find a cheap apartment located on the outer edge of the university's orbit. The apartment was just far enough away from the campus so that the neighborhood wasn't full of students. It wasn't that I didn't want to be a student. It was just that I didn't want to live among them. I wanted to live where it was quiet and where I could be alone.

The apartment had one large room and a hall which was wide enough to turn into a study. I put a double bed, two metal bookcases, two wooden chairs in the large room, and a large dining room table and my most comfortable chair in the hall. Although the apartment was crowded, it felt bigger to me because I didn't just use the hall to get to my room. In other apartments I've lived in since then, I've often filled them with chairs, because I am sure that makes them seem larger than they actually are. By moving from one chair to another, I can convince myself that one or two rooms are made up of many tiny ones, each a bubble containing its own atmosphere.

For most of that year I liked to stay up all night, reading and occasionally trying to hit one of the cockroaches that would suddenly scurry up the wall opposite me. The point was to hit the roach with a tennis ball and duck before the ball zinged back and hit me. I never did hit one of them, but I did get popped once or twice.

I suppose I felt it was okay to play this game because I could also be hit by the ball. I also imagined that one day, though it never did happen, that the ball could flatten the roach and then smack me, leaving some stain on my clothes. Somehow, all of this made the game fair or so I told myself. But actually, the game was a way of making sure I stayed awake.

The roaches would wait until they were sure I was deep in some book, and then one of them would make a mad dash up the wall toward the ceiling. Since there was no food on the ceiling, I was sure that they were not making some suicidal dash for supplies.

I usually picked up some movement out of the corner of my eye, and pretended to keep reading. I would sit, hunched over my book, and wait until the roach was out in the open and couldn't turn back; and then I would pick the ball off the floor, and heave it as hard as I could at the moving target.

If I was lucky, the roach plopped onto my table, ran around in circles, and then tried to parachute to safety. Some of them made it. Other times, I had to go into the bathroom, get some toilet paper, and wipe their messy remains off whatever book I was reading.

The game started to go wrong when, after I had been living there a few months, the roach population seemed to be increasing exponentially. It was as if my reading had become an unwanted interruption in the game, rather than the game being a grim but entertaining recess from reading. When this happened, I stopped playing and learned to

13

ignore them as they ran up and down the wall all night. There's a point when killing roaches is no longer fun, but a matter of efficiency that ends up leaving a bad taste in one's mouth. It was clear that the apartment was no longer mine, but ours.

Except for the number painted in gold on the etched glass of the front door, the building I lived in was largely indistinct from the other buildings on the block; it was six stories high and had a black-and-white tiled foyer with brass mailboxes lined up in two neat rows on each wall. Inside, the staircase and halls were dark and foreboding, and the wooden paneling and bannisters had long since turned the color of old meat.

My apartment was one of two at the end of a long hall on the first floor. Otherwise, the building seemed to have at least four apartments on every floor. Although I lived in the building for nearly a year, I only met two of the other tenants, a cheerful woman, Mrs. O'Connor, who lived on one of the upper floors, and the old woman who lived across the hall from me.

I tended to follow a schedule that isolated me from my classmates and even my friends. I went to bed around the time my first class was starting, and got up shortly after my last lecture was over. I would eat breakfast and read the paper in the late afternoon, and then once every few days I would walk or take a trolley down to the campus and go to the library. It was to return the books I had finished and borrow some more. I seldom stayed on the campus after I left the library.

In the evening, I would go out and walk around, mostly up and down the same streets. If the weather was warm enough, I would go to a nearby park and sit on a bench, smoke and daydream. Occasionally, on my way back to the apartment, I would stop in a bar filled with old men who rested on their stools, like slabs of dried mud.

When I was nearly broke, I would go over to Cambridge and try selling silver earrings I had learned how to make from an ex-girlfriend, Eva. There were a half dozen or so stores in Cambridge that took my earrings on consignment, and I was usually able to make enough money doing that to get by. I would only make a dozen or so pairs at one time, because I got bored and even a little depressed making the same sets over and over. I'm not very artistic so the five or six designs I came up with were relatively simple and easy to make. They looked good and people bought them, but I was always aware of what I couldn't do, rather than what I did.

My apartment faced an alley and got little light. It was grim and dark during the day, which was when I slept, but pleasant and quiet enough late at night, when I would sit in the hall and read. I ate at the same table, and, in the end, I probably spent most of my time there. Along with whatever books were piled on the table, there was a little transister radio and a phone that seldom rang.

I first met Mrs. O'Connor in the front foyer, and then ran into her on the street a few times after that. We always stopped and said hello. Although she was probably in her sixties and a widow, she was a robust, ruddy-faced woman with a trace of Irish brogue. We would usually chat about the weather, or I would say something innocuous about my classes. Early on, probably because I told Mrs. O'Connor my parents were born in China, she got it into her head that I was studying physics or math.

One Sunday evening, when I was on my way out, I saw Mrs. O'Connor standing in the foyer, face close to the glass, as if she were waiting for someone. After saying hello, she asked me if I knew the woman who lived across the hall from me. Both of them had, she told me, lived in this building for many years, and seen many people come and go.

I told Mrs. O'Connor I had only seen my neighbor once, when I was standing in the unlit hall, fumbling through my pockets, looking for my key. She had opened the door a crack and asked me if I was all right. Mrs. O'Connor smiled, but said nothing more, and I left the building.

I don't know why certain memories continue to rise to the surface, but they do. In my mind, the old woman and Mrs. O'Connor are one memory.

Another memory I have is of a cemetery on the outskirts of Butte, Montana, that is full of Chinese gravestones, many of which are made of wood. A friend of mine took me there once, when I went out to visit him and his wife. The gravestones tilted this way and that, like magazines in a newsstand at the end of a rainy day. I kept looking at the stones and wondering what had been written on them more than a hundred years ago. And yet, what I remember most about that graveyard was that on the way there, we drove past a jet mounted on a concrete pedestal, as if it were ascending into the sky above Butte, ready to do battle against the enemy. Although I went to Montana many years after I met Mrs. O'Connor, I know that somewhere in the atmosphere these two events are linked by something more than my momentary existence.

The only other people who knocked on my door that year were Jehovah's Witnesses. I don't know how any of them got into the building since the front door was locked and someone had to let them in, but a number of times I would be roused from whatever reverie or dream I was in by a loud but firm knocking on my door. After this happened a couple of times, I pretended no one was home until whoever it was gave up and went away.

One afternoon, it must have been on a Saturday or Sunday, I was sitting by my table and reading, when I heard someone knocking on my door. At first I ignored it because I was sure it was a Jehovah's Witness who had gotten into the building. But the knocking persisted, and I could hear a woman clearing her throat and then carefully but firmly mispronouncing my name. After a few moments I realized that it was my next door neighbor and got up and opened the door.

She was probably around the same age as Mrs. O'Connor, but was slighter and more delicate looking. If Mrs. O'Connor had once been a nurse, then my next door neighbor was the frail and eccentric old woman she took care of.

For some reason, my neighbor had put rouge on her deeply lined, pale cheeks, painted a wide slash of bright red lipstick on her thin lips, and was wearing high heels and a shiny maroon dress that seemed a little too big. She looked as if she were about to go to her high school prom fifty years too late. There was something ridiculous and sad about her; and it was easy to tell that she was afraid of something and thought that by dressing up she could protect herself. I was surprised by her appearance, but figured she was about to go out with friends and reminisce about the good old days.

I was just standing there, looking at her and wondering

what was going on, when I heard her say: "I thought since we were neighbors, I would invite myself over for a cup of tea."

I kept looking at her, unsure of exactly what to do next. Perhaps if I pretended that I didn't understand English, she would go away.

"You do have some tea, don't you?" she asked. "Chinese people drink tea, don't they? It doesn't matter if you're not Chinese because Japanese people also drink tea if I am not mistaken."

I mumbled something about my English grandmother and let her into my apartment.

I got a chair for her, cleared the stack of books off the table, and then went and rummaged through the kitchen. In one of the metal cupboards above the sink full of dirty dishes, I found a box of tea bags that Eva had left behind, along with a jar of honey and a couple of teacups. I also had some cookies, which I had bought a couple of nights earlier, and for some reason or another, I didn't get around to finishing.

I rinsed out a pot, put some water in it, placed it on the stove, and waited. I wasn't sure what else to do, and thought that maybe if I stayed in the kitchen long enough, my neighbor would get up and leave. However, from where I was standing, I could see that she was showing no signs of getting restless, and, a few minutes later, I brought everything into the hallway, where she was sitting calmly, like a customer who is sure the waiter will bring her exactly what she wants. Finally, when I was sure everything had been placed on the table, I sat down.

It seemed that all she wanted to do was tell someone her life story. For most of the time I could follow what she was saying. Her husband had died many years earlier, and they never had any children. Someone had given her a dog, a cocker spaniel named Arthur, but she had to give it away because it was too hard for her to take it out on a walk every day. She once worked as secretary to the vice-president of a shipping firm, and she and her husband had once driven as far as Phoenix, Arizona.

Every now and then, she would stop what she was saying, look at me strangely with her big, rheumy blue eyes, and then pick up her cup and take a little sip. A smear of lipstick formed on the rim, like a bruise. It was an awkward situation, but I figured an hour or two wouldn't matter, and that eventually she would leave on her own.

At some point everything changed. First, she looked at me, smiled briefly, and then started to act flustered. "Why are you looking at me like that?" she asked. It was more of a demand than a question. "What do you have up your filthy little sleeve, young man?"

I began to sit up straight.

"Who do you think you're kidding? Why I bet you're not even a citizen, that you're some kind of Commie spy. Hey buster, why are you trying to do this to me?"

A torrent of questions and accusations began to pour out of her, saliva collecting on her thin, bright red lips, until they glistened like a fire truck that has just been washed. Her eyes grew hard, cold, and shiny, as she began jabbing the air with a long, bony finger. She was the prosecutor and I was the defendant. I tried to remain calm, tried to change the subject, knowing it was pointless to do so.

Frightened by what could happen next, I said, "Maybe we should call up your friend, Mrs. O'Connor, and invite her down here. Wouldn't that be nice?"

For a brief moment the old woman seemed to relax, and settled back into her chair and nodded. Then, I said cheerfully, "You know I don't happen to have Mrs. O'Connor's phone number on me. Isn't that a shame?"

Having said this as calmly as possible, I didn't know what else to say. I suddenly stood up and bolted out of my apartment, leaving the door open. I ran to the front foyer and then stopped, wondering whom I should call and what I would say. It was sunny and warm outside, and a young couple walked by, hand in hand. I thought of interrupting them, but changed my mind. What was I going to tell them? "Excuse me, but could you help me? There's an elderly woman in my apartment and I can't seem to get her out of there."

I don't know how long I stood there, hoping Mrs. O'Connor would suddenly appear before me. But she didn't. No one did, and finally, after what seemed like a long time, I got up the courage and went back to my apartment.

The door was still open, but the old woman was gone. I closed the door, and, like a criminal who wants to leave no fingerprints behind, I quickly washed the dirty cups, saucers, silverware and plate, and threw open the kitchen window, because I could still smell the perfume she had been wearing. That night I just lay in the dark, like a condemned man waiting for dawn.

A few days later, I heard Mrs. O'Connor knocking softly on the door. She stood in the hall, looking a little less robust and cheerful than usual, and told me that my neighbor had been taken to a hospital and probably wouldn't be coming back to her apartment. I didn't need to ask what kind of hospital and Mrs. O'Connor didn't feel she had to tell me. Although Mrs. O'Connor never made any mention of the incident, she must have known that something strange had happened between me and my neighbor in my apartment. How she found out about it I will never know, though I suspect the woman across the hall may have done something similar to Mrs. O'Connor. After she finished, she reached out, patted me on the arm and said, "You've been a good boy. The best of luck to you."

It was the first time and only time I saw her walking with her head down, and it was one of the last times we talked.

All this happened many years ago and I'm sure both women are now dead. I don't know what Mrs. O'Connor's friends called her and I never learned the name of the woman who lived across the hall. After I graduated from college, I moved around quite a lot before finally settling in Manhattan. And now, whenever I'm on my way to Chinatown to buy some groceries or meet a friend for dinner, I wonder about all the old men and women who are hurriedly crossing Canal Street, as if no one is in front of them. They look right through me, as if I'm a glass door that will automatically open for them. But, for reasons that must by now be obvious, I don't mind that they act like they don't see me. After all, I'm just another foreigner in their midst.

A New Set of Rules Every Other Day

Social Studies
Some girls said they wouldn't kiss me because I wasn't black. Others said it was because I wasn't white. And still others kissed me because they were sure I was an exotic plant in need of constant tending.

Geography
There are two Chinas. One is a large blank spot on the map and in text books. The other is only mentioned in passing.

Mythology
They are studious, quiet, and well-behaved. They wear glasses and white socks, pants that are too short, and dresses that are too long. The smartest ones major in math or physics. They never go out for sports. They tend to have poor eyesight and buck teeth. They talk funny, and can't tell left from light.

Rumors

Six guys on the football team supposedly fuck her on a pool table, in the alley behind the liquor store, or on the baseball field at midnight. She wears dresses, nylons, and low heels. A thin gold necklace and pale pink lipstick. A quiet girl who seems to have no friends, she sits at the back of the classroom and stares out the window. She once told the girl sitting next to her that her parents owned a laundry in a nearby town, and that she was an only child. The other students begin looking at her differently, noticing perhaps for the first time how pretty she is, but no one tries to find out what, if anything, happened.

Image

I look like one, but I don't act like one.

First Rule of Romance

If you tell anyone, even your best friend, what you and your girlfriend did at the movies, then you are advertising what she will do for someone else.

True Love

I can't let you fuck me. You can put your fingers inside me, but that's all. I have a boyfriend, and I want to stay faithful to him.

Friendship

Baker screams: "Don't anyone talk about my sister that way." He's fuming over the whispers he imagines are following him around, like hungry dogs.

24

Each of us is remembering what Doug had said when he entered the schoolyard a few minutes before Baker: "Hey you know what happened to Dolly? She's got one baking in the oven. Must've been Frankie didn't use no safe. Man oh man, is her dad pissed."

Crush

"Why are you walking with Louella? Don't you like me?"

I drop back from the group, and begin walking beside Caroline. We slow down, surreptitiously hold hands, and begin whispering about the other kids. Caroline has a blonde pony tail and warm blue eyes. The small silver braces on her front teeth look like rings an elf might wear.

Caroline tells me her father is a Colonel in the army, and that before moving here she lived in Paris and Berlin. A few days later, when she brings me home, her mother, who is sure that I will not understand what she's saying, begins speaking in French.

"Who is this boy? Why did you bring him home?"

Parental Advice

When I tell my mother about what happened when I went to Caroline's house that afternoon, she gives me her stock answer: "You don't want to get involved with a girl like that. She'll become dependent on you and won't let you alone. Remember, she's not as smart as you."

Later, during dinner, my father doesn't look up from his bowl when he issues his opinion: "I don't see what she sees in you. If you ask me, she's one dumb duck."

My mother's head bobs, like a pigeon's. It's the first

time in years my parents have found something they agree upon.

Secret Meeting
We lie in the dirt and kiss each other so hard, it's as if we are trying to merge and become someone else, someone who doesn't have parents and doesn't go to school.

A Lesson in the Meaning of Time
One afternoon, I'm caught smoking on the roof of my school and given twenty-five hours of detention. The next day, after classes are over, I show up for detention a few minutes late. The other offenders are already seated, pretending to be busy. The teacher orders me to sit down and read a book. I pull my reading matter out of my back pocket and wave it in front of his face.

"See, it says 'book' right here." I point to the word, tap it with my finger, as if to prove I'm holding a solid object.

"Comic book," I say slowly, as if I'm just learning to speak English. "Yes, it says, B-O-O-K. Pletty good book, too. Don't you stink?"

The teacher sends me to the principal, who says: "Don't you know all Chinese kids are well behaved, good students? What's wrong with you? I should tell your parents. They'll know what to do with you. You sit over there, and keep your eyes on the clock. I'll tell you when you can go home."

For the next three weeks, I spend three hours a day learning how to sleep while sitting up with my eyes open.

Friendship
The kids at the schoolyard call me Zero. Students of history, they are thinking of the plane, red circles on each wing. "Rat-a-tat-tat," they say as I pass them in the hall. When I get into a fight, they gather around and make bets as to who will win.

"If you lose, Zero, you lose twice," a bunch of kids yell, waving dollar bills in the air.

Social Studies
There are two brothers and one sister. They live with their father in a small apartment overlooking the trolley tracks.

"On the wrong side, of course," Matt points out, when we go to his house one afternoon.

The turn-of-the-century tenement is at one end of a parking lot, which is adjacent to the tracks leading to the city. Once part of a row of tenements, the dilapidated, brick building now stands alone, a forgotten guardhouse on the border between one neighborhood and another.

A dense but invisible cloud of familiar smells — garlic, ginger, and fermented black beans — greets us when Matt opens the front door.

Matt's father is sitting in the kitchen, by the window. The walls are painted a color which falls somewhere between hospital cafeteria and failed biology experiment. The floor is covered with linoleum, a blue and yellow pattern of scuffed triangles. Gray lace curtains and streaked windows that rattle each time the trolley passes.

Round wooden table, crumpled pack of cigarettes, full ashtray.

Matt's father looks at me as if I am not there. No nod, no smile. I might as well be the dirty window he was gazing through, daydreaming about a life that has started slipping out of his control. The reason Matt's father is silent is not because he is shy or because he doesn't understand English. He is a waiter and knows enough English to get by. He is brooding because his wife left him two months ago and he is sure his children know where she went and are planning to join her.

Matt and his father begin speaking Cantonese, which I don't understand.

"Who is he?" his father asks. "Why have you brought him into my house?"

"He is a friend," Matt answers quickly. "Don't worry, we'll be leaving soon. I just needed to get something."

Later, Matt tells me all this, but otherwise says little about his parents.

Mythology

My mother, who is from Shanghai, tells me that when a person speaks Cantonese, he sounds like he is imitating a dog who has a stomach ache. After she finishes her pronouncement, she raises the bowl piled high with food to her mouth, and uses her chopsticks to slurp down more food.

Nicknames

Sneak Attack, Kamikaze, Banzai, General Toe Jam.

Parental Discretion is Advised

At home, my mother, who thinks white people are descendants of apes, says unequivocally: "They have hair on their bodies." This, she makes clear, is the essential lesson in biology I must memorize, the one that will get me into college.

"It's proof that they haven't evolved very much," my mother, the Neo-Darwinian, concludes.

I am sitting in the kitchen, watching my mother make dinner. I want to tell her that she is married to a man who is half English, and that, according to her logic, her husband is part gorilla, but I am sure she will agree with my conclusion, will act as if her logic is unimpeachable, and that it is me who has to learn the truth of the world and its ways.

Mythology
They trap and eat pigeons from the park. They scoop up cats from street corners and alleys, cook and serve them in restaurants.

Family Life
My mother likes to point out that my father never learned to write in Chinese. "It's a sign of his ignorance," she whispers to me, as if he is behind the door, listening.

Census
There are no Japanese families living in town, a fact which those in the nickname business have never learned. To them, all Asians are both Chinese and Japanese, there is no difference. They are merely something to laugh at.

Friendship
One day, during my junior year, Matt, his brother, Billy, and sister, Pearl, disappear. The money Matt's father kept under the mattress is gone. Soon, Miss Quincy, our home

room teacher, takes roll call without calling out Matt's name, without looking up to see if he might be sitting at his desk. It's as if Matt has never sat in this room, has never stood up in the morning and said the Pledge of Allegiance.

For the next few weeks the cops stop me on the street, tell me to get in the back of the car, and take me to Matt's house. They escort me inside, stand on either side, and one of them knocks on the door. The father, who is always there, looks at me in disgust, and shakes his head emphatically.

"That's not him, that's someone else," he says to the officers, who don't seem embarrassed by their mistake.

Even though these are the only times I hear Matt's father speak English, he always acts as if he's never met me before. After he closes the door and goes back to his chair by the window, the cops and I go downstairs without saying anything. Out on the street, they stop and look at me a little closer, and then get in their car and drive away.

The Distance Between Home Plate and First Base
"Hey, would you like a ride?" Toni asks. I nod, and get in her purple and white 1959 Chevy convertible. Ten blocks later, she drops me off on the corner, near the bookstore.

Two days later, Henry walks over to me in the school cafeteria. "Toni's got a crush on you. Touch her and you're dead meat, Zero. She's one of ours."

A few tables away, a bunch of other boys are watching, elbowing each other, and smiling.

Henry leans over, a big grin cutting across the bottom of his pimply face, pushes his finger into my chest. "You got that, you longhaired, scum sucking, fuckface," he says through clenched teeth, practically spitting the words out at me.

Meaningful Encounter

The star outfielder of the local baseball team is receiving an award in the high school auditorium. It's Saturday night and most everyone has downed a couple of beers in the parking lot before entering the building. Shrill echoes bounce down the poorly lit, basement hallways, while the animated shuffle of adolescent boys hurriedly climbing metal stairs fills the stairwells and corridors with an unlikely sense of excitement. It is sounds like these the teachers believe they have to banish during the week.

I'm in the lavatory, standing at the urinal, when four cops stride in and tell all the kids but me to leave. They line up on either side of me, as another cop, a big, burly sergeant, walks in and stands behind me. The sergeant pushes his night stick into my back, and I fall forward, getting my sneakers wet, but I don't protest. What do they want? I have to find out what they want or know before I say anything.

"What were you doing this afternoon around 3:00?"

"Excuse me."

"You heard me, what were you doing at 3:00?"

"I was at home, watching TV."

"Really."

"Yes sir."

"Well, we have a witness that says you and a couple of other kids were breaking windows over at the elementary school. You wouldn't know anything about that, would you?"

"No sir."

"The witness says there were three of you. We know you were one of them. What happened? Did the others make you do it? Did they dare you?"

I don't say anything.

"Look, we know you're not a troublemaker. I've been

a cop twenty years and I've never seen a Chinese kid get in trouble before. So just give us their names. They won't know you told us. I promise. They'll never know."

In Search of Beauty
"I know one thing, that's for sure. I'll never go out with an oriental."
"An oriental?"
"Yeah, an oriental. There's no such thing as a pretty oriental girl. Didn't you know that?"

Anthropology
I'm on my way home one afternoon when I see Marlene knocking on the window and motioning me to come in. She introduces me to her guitar teacher, Celeste, who stands up and shakes my hand. I notice that she is considerably shorter than I am, and that she is wearing lipstick and high heels.

At lunch the next day, Marlene comes over to me and whispers: "Celeste thinks you're cute."

"Are you crazy?" I ask, convinced that Marlene and her friends are setting some kind of trap, since Celeste is at least twenty five and I'm only sixteen, and we are from different places on the planet.

Marlene nods thoughtfully. "No, I'm not crazy, but she is about you. You should stop by around 5:00. That's when Celeste finishes her last lesson."

One evening, a few weeks later, while walking down the street toward my parent's house, I hear someone call my name and stop and turn around. I see Celeste getting out of her car. Leaving the door open, she walks toward me, smiling. It's a warm spring night. She's wearing a tight white blouse with big buttons, a pleated blue skirt, nylons, and high heels. My heart's thumping so loud I can barely hear myself think.

"Where are you going in such a hurry? Maybe I can give you lift," she asks in a friendly, casual sort of way.

"Oh nowhere really," I answer, knowing that I am being honest if dumb.

"It's a nice night, isn't it?" she says. "Maybe, if you aren't going anywhere, we could take a drive, go up the hill, look at the city. It's always so peaceful up there. I love looking at the city from up there, don't you?" she asks, knowing she has invited me to cross a line with her.

"Yeah, it's really nice up there around now," I answer, sure that I hadn't quite said it right.

After sitting in the car, and gazing at the city for a few minutes, Celeste says, "Let's get in back. It's more comfortable."

We sit next to each other, and, after a few long, awkward seconds, we begin kissing. I'm nervous and excited. Suddenly, she puts her hand on my chest, leans over and whispers in my ear, "wait."

Am I rushing? I don't think so. Besides, I am not even sure what I am rushing toward?

Celeste brushes her hair out of her face, and smiles. We are sitting at an angle, facing each other, close. She inches back, pulls up her skirt. White garter belt, dark brown bands of her nylons, smooth thighs, pink underpants. She takes my hand and places it between her thighs.

Do I know what to do? Do I know how? Or when?

I realize there's a chorus of voices rumbling around in my head. All of them are offering detailed advice, none of which is informative. I try ignoring them because I am convinced there are only three options. Celeste shows me what to do. I do something. I jump over what she wants and force myself on her.

I learn that there is a fourth.

Celeste leans her head on my shoulder and begins talking, with my hand between her legs, my palm against her crotch, my fingers curving under it. As I feel her body shift and then relax, I start rubbing my palm against her, move my fingers slowly, tentative, unsure of what I'm doing, but sensing from her reaction that this is what she wants. By this time, her legs are resting on my lap, my other arm is around her shoulder, and we are starting to slide sideways. She looks up and smiles.

"You know, I thought you were an Indian when I first saw you. A beautiful Indian warrior."

A Little Memento from the Boys

There were three of us; Johnny Yamamoto, Virgo Van Dyke, and me. We all met each other a few months earlier in Mike's Last Dive, a bar in Tribeca which, before loft buildings became fashionable residences for dentists, movie stars, and other members of the upper echelons of the service industry, was where artists, would-be artists and others, like myself, lived. Most of us were at the bottom end of the service industry, the ones who plastered or plumbered by day, and painted or wrote at night.

Mike's Last Dive was a decaying, turn-of-the-century bar with sawdust on the floor. It had one pool table in the center of its square, high-ceilinged room, like a brightly lit, grass-covered, traffic island at night, long lines of cars rushing by. There was a long, narrow bathroom that smelled as if grizzled whalers used to line up and piss there. A sweet, sickly smell of disinfectant, urine, cigarettes, and stale beer had soaked into the bathroom's tile walls, tin ceiling, and wooden floor. I felt like I was pissing in a cold cave or a decrepit refrigerator.

Mike and his brother Ethan ran the place, and were

35

somewhere between seventy-five and a hundred. They had less teeth than most infants, but only occasionally drank directly from a bottle, usually beer.

The only decoration in Mike's Last Dive was a frayed marlin someone had mounted on the wall above the bar, its dark wood shelves stocked with bottles. A string of red and green Christmas lights, tinsel, and silver and blue teardrop ornaments dangled from its dusty mouth. No one remembered who put the marlin up or why it had been wrapped in lights and Christmas decorations, and no one ever thought of changing it. The regulars called the marlin Uncle Bill for some reason or another. If no one knew who was batting champion in the American League in 1953, everyone chimed in "ask Uncle Bill."

Late one night, Johnny, Virgo, and I kept crossing each other's paths on the way to the toilet or, while standing and watching some of the regulars playing pool, we'd look up and see a face looking back, curious. We began checking each other out, circling each other, slowly, like animals in heat.

Why did we begin talking? Well, the obvious reason is that we immediately recognized that we were mongrels, confused children whose parents came from different worlds, which in our cases meant Asia and Europe. We were what was left after the collision; we were the things they had dropped on the floor.

Shortly after the fires that swept across the world died down, our parents emigrated from some smoky crater in Asia to America, Canada, and Costa Rica. At first they were stalked by the ghosts of their past, and were afraid of the shadows lurking in the corners of their future. Eventually, they developed routines which helped them adjust, made them seem like they were part of the pattern. They became an accountant, a research scientist, and an engineer. They held jobs with no public visibility. They lived in a zone drained of light by the past, squeezed of money by the present, and stared at by the disapproving future. They sat at tiny desks and wondered when history would leave them alone.

Their eldest children became loners by default. They can't seem to find a group that will take them in, that they can run with. They don't feel quite at home with anyone, even themselves. We're those children, the ones who smirk inwardly, but now we're in our twenties, drinking in different bars in downtown Manhattan, a few blocks from Wall Street and those who believe that home is wherever they can go and spend other people's money.

Each night, Johnny, Virgo, and I tell stories about what it is like to be regarded as a Martian by those who claim to be our friends. It's as if we have to tell all the stories lodged inside our chests so as to never have to tell them again, to each other or ourselves.

"My father's Japanese, my mother's German," Johnny states with a diplomat's flair. "The worst of both worlds. I grew up speaking Spanish."

"You want to know what it's like to have a Dutch name but slanted eyes?" Virgo asks. It is a question he has asked and answered in many different ways.

"You want to know what my fourth grade teacher said to me on the first day of class? She asked me if I had been adopted," Virgo says softly, his voice bordering on a hiss.

"Oh yes," I tell her. "When I was born, Mrs. Pringle, my parents decided it would be better if they gave me away, but got some money in return. You see my enlightened parents wanted to open a fancy Chinese restaurant in downtown

Vancouver, that was their lifelong dream. When I was born, Mrs. Pringle, they saw their one and only chance at redemption and bundled me and took me into town. There, they sold me to a nice old Dutch guy who rolled cigars. His wife made me these wooden shoes." Heels click together in the din of voices, a hand rises in phony salute. "Yes, Mrs. Plingle, this is why I'm so well behaved."

We snicker and guffaw in agreement. Virgo's glad he finally has friends who will knowingly roll each morsel and crumb of his offerings around on their tongues, lick their lips, and hoot and howl for more. We are ravenous dogs who gather in this noisy room each night, and tell more tales. No meat is too tough for us to tear from the bone. We're coyotes who've wandered into a ghost town.

Sometimes Johnny would look at me and smile, and I knew what was coming. "You got English and Chinese parents, the best of both worlds. You got two fucking histories to live up to, while I got two to live down. Ha."

"Yeah, right. You a scrawny samurai and me a gimp coolie," I answer. And all three of us laugh.

Best, worst, up, and down. There is no middle ground, no safe place for us in the world, no belief that will take us in, soothe us. We live on the poison we secrete. We spend our nights characterizing ourselves in derogatory terms. It is the only defense we know. Our motto: Beat them to the punch, before they beat you to a pulp.

Every night, we drink until we are standing on our heads and the world is melting like a candle, blue and red neon tears running down dirty walls, dusty windows, and dank warehouses full of a century of crud. Whalers' bones and broken phones. Dusty trunks and lumpy bunks.

After Mike or Ethan announce last call, we go and stand outside in the cool night air, pointing at the people trying to cling to the moon and broken streetlights, afraid now that gravity has gathered them up and delivered them to the deck of a storm-tossed ocean liner. A slippery world with no safe place to stand and nothing to grab onto. It is the only time we feel at home.

To us the young Wall Street types are all the same. A bunch of well-groomed, faceless young men, who took off their suit jackets when they played pool and thought they were entitled to talk to every woman who drifted in through the doors alone. They were sure that money gave them the power to be at home wherever they went, and fervently believed that they are on their way to heaven, not on their way out the door and down the chute.

The ups and the outs, that's how I saw the world. Those were the only two real places on the map, the rest was an illusion, the place where the earth finally becomes an edge and the little sailing ship falls forever.

Johnny, Virgo, and I learned to lower our anger to a slow but steady flame. Each night we sidled up to it with alcohol, saw how close we could come to it without having the bombs go off in our faces. That was our power, coming as close to the ticking heart as possible, and still being able to lift the drinks, one after another, with a cool, disinterested hand, a hand that could belong to someone else, someone who was dead, someone whose muscles only moved when the electric volts punched in their white hot charge.

I don't know who came up with the idea first, probably Johnny, who hadn't had a job in nearly two months, but we all agreed it was a quick, sure way to make some money. Sand floors, paint walls, and plaster. We would help the people we hated move into Tribeca, and then, if we were smart and lucky, we would move on. Go to San Francisco, Los Angeles, Paris, Rio, or Berlin. Somewhere, we told ourselves, there was a city and a bar where we could dream about the future, rather than keep returning to the past.

I doubt if any of us saved money that year. I doubt if we believed there was anywhere we could go. Paradise was a glitzy bar six blocks away, but we preferred Mike's Last Dive. It was our watering hole, our oasis. We could have found it blindfolded, that's how deep it was lodged in our souls.

We usually worked from eleven in the morning to around seven or eight o'clock at night, sometimes later. Then we headed off to our separate apartments, washed the dust off our bodies, squeezed the ache out of our muscles, changed, and met up around ten or midnight. Then life began.

Eating and drinking. Often just drinking. Scoring some dope, smoking it. Then eating and drinking. Taking pills, smoking dope, and drinking. Lots of loud music. Swallowing, snorting, smoking, and drinking. Washing the dust from our brains.

The next morning was always the same. I tried pulling my body off the bed and onto the floor. A poor specimen of human desire, I tried to maintain an erect position, tried not to crash into the table or wall. I wobbled like a gyroscope winding down, trying desperately to speed up and get my balance again. I washed, then dressed. It was all an act of memory. I went out, bought coffee, met the others, rented equipment, and went to the job. Began sanding or painting. Finished, I would stumble home, wash the outside, then go out and wash the inside. An act of cleansing. A merry-go-round.

Sometimes I fell asleep on the floor, a prone body wearing a face mask, passed out in the corner of a big, empty white room, sweat soaking through my shirt, and feeling the cool floor beneath me. It was almost erotic, lying there on the floor, clouds of sawdust rising all around you, the entire room vibrating to the steady hum of Johnny or Virgo pushing a sander up and down the floor. Magic fingers, I thought to myself before drifting off. Oh warm magic fingers, take me away from this world.

Lila is one of the people who hired us after hearing about what we did from Lola, her downstairs neighbor and one of our earliest employers. She lived alone on the top floor of a bird-stained loft building in Soho.

"I work in the record industry, I'm a sound mixer," she said the first night we met her. "I can make the trumpets turn into honey. I'm the reason you hear what you do."

Johnny, Virgo, and I were at her place to see what had to be done, as well as discuss money. Lila was wearing a red satin jacket, tight black stretch pants, and a shiny black silk blouse that clung to her like Saran wrap. She had long black hair which she tied into a knot above her head. Strands dangled down and framed her pale oval face. She looked like a cross between Pebbles Flintstone and the girl everyone in high school used to whisper puts out, as if they had actually benefited from or been threatened by her generosity.

Lila was staring at us with disdain. We were looking at her as if she were a cute but full piggybank, something to break open and rob. We wanted her paper and her coin, something negotiable, not her body, which, athletic and attractive as it was, Johnny, Virgo, and I had learned to live without.

Lila was either on her way out or just got in, and Johnny, Virgo, and I were standing there, telling her we'd be honored to sand her floors, paint her walls, move her furniture, such as it was, out of the way.

Yes, we'd gladly and lovingly get down on our knobby knees and lick your toes, kiss your shoes. Just give us two hundred and fifty dollars a day to divide among us, and we'll be out of here in a week. In return, your floors and walls will glisten like television teeth.

To our surprise, Lila agreed to it. She was going to be in LA for ten days on business, and wanted everything done by the time she got back. We waited until we were out the door and charging down the stairs before we started grinning. It was the most money we had ever gotten from anyone.

It started out as an easy job and we finished a lot of the basic stuff in the first few days. Once the floors of both rooms were sanded, we started painting the walls.

I don't know why we didn't notice it right away, but we didn't. Anyway, the second time Johnny and Virgo moved Lila's bed, I, for some reason or another, probably pure nosiness, pulled back the bedspread, its silkscreened images of Elvis's record covers.

"Holy shit, that's the biggest fucking vibrator I've ever seen." Johnny was the first to notice it.

It had been lying under her black satin pillow.

"You're right. I thought it was a flashlight or something," I say.

"That's no flashlight," Virgo exclaims. "Man, I've

never seen one so big. A flashlight that big would be illegal. Why, it would be declared a dangerous weapon. Hell, man, it's big enough to be a dildo for lonely girl elephants."

"You've actually seen one of these things before?" I ask. I was a bit incredulous. Where had Virgo seen a vibrator before? I mean up close, not on the other side of a window in a store in the Village.

"Yeah, my little sister, Denise, has one," he says matter-of-factly. "I saw it the last time I visited her in Vancouver."

"Hmmmmmmm," Johnny says, trying to sound like a motor.

At first, we stand there staring at it, as if it was the Christ Child lying in the manger, and we're the three Wisemen. Hey, look what we brought you, when actually it's the other way around and we know it. Lila is giving us more than money, she's giving us one of her secrets. But we're greedy and want more, because we're tired of our own secrets.

We begin laughing, nervous at first, then we grow silently curious about whether she has a diary or not, whether she may have written something revealing in its pages. Does it, we are thinking, have a name. Ralph or Max, maybe? The Long and Mighty Dumbo and his electric nightstick? We're stuck in a kaleidoscope, but this time we believe it's Lila's and not ours.

It didn't take long for us to begin going through her things, pulling open drawers, checking the closet, opening boxes. We found it on a shelf, tucked away behind some books. Her leather-bound diary.

We spend the rest of the afternoon taking turns reading it aloud, the other two guys holding long poles, and rolling the white paint up and down the walls, trying not to break stride. Little tears of milk slurping down the walls.

Lila likes to keep a running record of her sexual fantasies. Near as we can figure it, she uses the vibrator on the average of twice a day when she is working and up to four times a day on weekends. The diary is filled with descriptions, some carefully printed in purple ink, others hastily written in pencil. One scrawl in maroon lipstick is smudged and illegible.

There's the garage mechanic who fixed her car, a young blonde lead guitarist, the quiet saxophonist who played backup on the third cut of a big hit album, the messenger who stopped and asked for directions, someone seen in the street, her best friend's boyfriend and his best friend at the same time, Clark Gable, Paul Newman, and Mick Jagger — she has had them all, more than once. Different combinations, contraptions, and situations.

"Lila's kind of like a Chinese menu," Virgo says after reading some more pages.

"Yeah," Johnny chimes in. "Choose one from column A and two from column B. A little duck sauce for my breasts, a little mustard for my thighs. And don't forget to bring me my big fortune cookie."

Johnny and I laugh and continue painting. The afternoon swirls away. Blue shadows fill the valley of the narrow streets, while the factories and loading docks grow silent.

It's the last day of the job. We've gotten to Lila's early for once, finished sanding and painting, and are cleaning up, putting everything back in place. Around noon, we break for lunch, go out and get sandwiches, chips, and cold cans of soda. Back in the loft, we sit on the floor and begin eating.

After we're finished, I pull out a joint, light up, and start passing it around. Johnny picks the diary off the floor, and, "for old time's sake," begins reading some of the parts we've liked the best. Virgo lays back on the floor, a joint stuck in his mouth, and stares at the ceiling, like a child listening to a bedtime story.

"Hey," Johnny says suddenly. "Remember that camera we found, you think there's any film in it?"

"I'll go look," I say, getting up and walking to the other room, knowing something good is about to take place.

Virgo sits up, a grin tattooed to his face.

For some reason, which I've never been able to understand, we were all ready to do the same thing.

"There's twelve shots left," I announce in my best Betty Davis voice, sashaying back into the room, camera dangling from my left hand.

"Shit, I got a great idea." Johnny is always having great ideas. "Why don't we jerk off into our last can of paint and touch up the place with it?"

"Huh?" I answer, realizing this is not exactly what I expected to happen, but I was more than ready to do. I'm looking at the camera, trying to figure out how it works.

Virgo is sitting up and sniffing the last of the smoke. He turns and looks at me. "Hey, that's a great idea," he says enthusiastically. "Let me see that camera. I bet I can set it on automatic so that it will take a picture of us jerking off. Won't that be a hoot?"

After we get everything set up, which we do in a hurry, as if all of us are being pulled forward by some unseen magnet, we jerk off into our last can of white paint, three men in their twenties. It's like the fervent gathering of a prayer group with Johnny leading the way. When we

45

get close, which somehow, miraculously, we all do at the same time, Virgo hobbles over to the camera and pushes the red button down and then hobbles back in time to rejoin us.

"Say cheese," we sing in unison.

Later, each of us has his picture taken holding the vibrator as if it is an ice cream cone. We sit and stand around like twelve-year-olds: licking our lips, sticking out our tongues, grinning into the camera. Twelve pictures, twelve poses. Then we finish the job, the last of the paint gone by the time we leave Lila's loft, white, shiny and smooth as a brand new refrigerator.

Johnny, Virgo, and I sanded more floors and painted more walls, but the job had started becoming a drudge after Lila's loft. We didn't find vibrators or diaries hidden beneath bedspreads, behind books, or in drawers, though we always looked before starting to paint. We didn't learn about other people's secrets, and we remained stuck with our own, the ones we kept telling each other, because to us they weren't secrets, but things other people didn't know or recognize. Worst of all, we weren't painters and sanders anymore. We were voyeurs stuck looking at walls, rather than through someone's window.

Hey, Lila, we thought we'd leave you a little something to remember us by.

Hey, Lila, we didn't want to just be three shadows passing through your busy, important life.

Hey, Lila, do you ever wake up in the middle of the night and feel like you're stuck inside a giant condom?

Hey, Lila, there's three mongrels out here, somewhere in America, who have drifted into different orbits. But they still have one thing in common: their sperm mixed in the paint covering your walls.

Hey, Lila, it's okay if you went out and hired someone to paint them over. It's even okay if your walls are now blue or pink or gray, because the sperm is still there, beneath whatever you have done.

Yes, Lila, thousands of frozen little creatures surround you and your lover, or whoever is waking up in that sunlit room now. And no matter what you do to them, no matter how many times you cover them over, they'll still be there, burrowing their way to the surface.

I'm sure Johnny and Virgo would understand why you wished those photographs had never left the little black Japanese box they were in, why you wished you never took the roll into the store and had it developed. Did the man say anything to you when he handed you the envelope? Or did he just smile? as if everything were okay.

Yes, the curly-haired, garage mechanic's big hands are still preserved like butterfly wings in your diary. It's the place where, each time you remember him, he is born between your long athletic legs. But wishing a person or a thing was never born, that's why Johnny, Virgo, and I did what we did. We wanted a different kind of diary, one that was written permanently on a wall where everybody could read it. It's why we took the pictures. We wanted someone to know who and what we had been.

A New Beginning

I had a job interview the next afternoon and needed to buy some new clothes. My girlfriend was at work and I was on my own. I went to the bank shortly before it closed and took out one hundred and forty dollars. That left twenty-eight in the account and a few hours to kill before I headed for the stores.

A hundred and forty dollars, seven crisp twenties. It was the most money I had had in my pocket since I had a job washing dishes the first summer after high school. I still remember my first pay check: Forty-nine dollars, forty-seven cents for forty-eight hours a week. It was the first steady job I had and it was nearly the last.

I'm thinking: What kind of clothes? A sports jacket, white shirt, and tie. Maybe some shoes. Pants, definitely pants. A suit, could I buy a suit? No, I couldn't buy a suit. I had never bought a suit. My mother bought me a suit once, a shiny black thing, when I was about to graduate from the eighth grade and enter high school. I hated it, wore it for the class photograph, and then stuck it in the closet, where it is still collecting dust next to my boy scout uniform. Hated that too. Wouldn't wear it either, and got myself thrown out.

A sports jacket, how do you buy a sports jacket?

I didn't know these things then. I thought buying clothes was a sign of failure, an admission that you wanted to join the hamster division of the human race and spend your days running inside a wheel.

A friend of mine, who had also spent his nights and days in bars, staggering into walls, sleeping on the floor, because the bed was too far from the front door, once told me: "The worst thing about being a drunk is you never buy shoes that fit. I didn't know that until I was sober, I thought my feet were supposed to hurt. I thought the pain was some kind of necessary proof, that it connected me to the earth."

Sneakers, dungarees, denim shirt, black leather jacket —not the clothes you wear to a job interview, not if you want to get the job. My girlfriend and I lived in a big unheated loft in Chinatown then, and I was walking around Lower Manhattan, telling myself: It's easy, you just walk in the store and pick out what you want. But I didn't know what I wanted, I didn't have the tiniest iota of a clue. A sports jacket. I might as well have been taking an exam in physics, it was that abstract to me.

Did I go into more than one bar or was it just that one? The Doll Pit, a seedy topless bar for delivery boys, truck drivers, security guards, post office employees, and, sometimes, the Wall Street, baby-faced, junior execs that ventured that far north during lunch hour or wanted to kill an hour or two after work, swell their chests up and flex their muscles before going home to their studios or one bedroom apartments filled with examples of all the right things in it.

50

The Doll Pit lived up to its name. It was an all-black room with a horseshoe bar, a small, mirrored runway for the dancers and a loud, blinking jukebox full of disco. Music for undulators, shakers, twisters, teasers, and, as I called them back then, the bunny robots. It was a theater with a ramshackle stage and an audience peppered with guys that would have been shooed away from the Roman Forum.

The layers of encrusted black paint soaked up all the daylight that managed to crawl under the thick black front door, made it hard to see how dirty it actually was in there. There was a frayed red carpet around the bar, though it looked like someone had poured a mixture of cabbage and old confetti on the floor. A gold-framed mirror stretched across the black wall behind the bar so the audience got simulvision, front and back views of the dancers. There was beer on tap and the hard liquor was under the bar.

If you were smart, you didn't ask for anything by brand name. Knowing the name of a liquor meant you were smart enough to have graduated from college and gotten a good job, but stupid enough to pay extra on top of the extra the bartender already charged you.

It's dumb to walk into a topless bar if you have a hundred and forty dollars in your pocket, twenty-eight in the bank, and no steady job. It's even dumber if you go there in the middle of the afternoon. The drinks cost more than in a regular bar. Even the beer costs more. You start drinking in the cool cave of a topless bar in the afternoon and suddenly, like Dracula, you know you have lots of time staring down at you.

I knew all the topless bars in Lower Manhattan and how late they stayed open. I also knew about the bars that didn't have names and opened their doors at midnight or later. The ones that stayed open until 9:00 a.m. I drank in bars where beautiful transvestites lip-synched to Page, Minelli and Streisand, and I drank in darker ones where firemen danced with waiters and cab drivers. I didn't discriminate. If they served alcohol, I'd go there. But midnight was a long way off and I had to buy a sports jacket, a tie, shirt, and shoes. It was a Herculean labor. I figured a couple of beers and a few naked dancers would smooth the way.

I didn't notice the sun go down. There was no window and you don't think about those kinds of things when you're sitting in a topless bar, swilling down beer or bourbon or both, watching bored women bouncing around, shaking their breasts as if they were frogs attached to batteries.

If you do do any thinking in a topless bar, which is hard to imagine given what the place is called, it's in the third person. He, you think to yourself. He can and he will when he wants to. He, it is clear to me now, didn't know how and couldn't admit it.

I was proud of the fact that I was drinking slow and steady, like a submarine sneaking up on its target, and still had most of my money in my pocket. The only plan I had when I went to the bank that afternoon was to hold onto enough money until it was dark. I knew I wanted to buy my clothes after the sun went down, but I wasn't sure why.

One of my favorite ways of communing with nature back then was to drink as much as I possibly could as fast as I could. It made me understand the laws of gravity on a cellular level. I could feel cosmic particles drifting through the vast, empty regions of my brain. I was sure I could hear the little explosions of surplus activity in my veins. Lying in a park, more than once I fell asleep on a bench or under it, I swear I could feel the earth tilting toward or away from the sun.

When you're drunk, you slip, if you're lucky, into a different form of motion, and dance on the ribbon between the laws of gravity and the parapets of imagination.

I was a Sufi pressed between the smoky pages of alcohol, a genie waiting to jump back into the bottle. I wanted to find the amber snake whose fangs were full of sweet, sweet poison. Well, this Sufi must have been dancing somewhere behind his eyes when she came up and asked me if I could give her change for a dollar, because she needed to use the phone. I handed her some change, watched her hand slide the dollar onto the bar, watched her walk off to the phone.

Dark brown pony tail, white cotton blouse, red Dacron skirt, nylons, and low, black patent leather heels. A familiar type; the office worker. Miss Pony Tail was probably a secretary in one of the buildings a few blocks further south, down toward the World Trade Center. Most likely, she lived in Queens or Brooklyn. Maybe Staten Island. She was short but not overweight. She had a figure, I could see that. What's she doing in a place like this? Oh well, I didn't even see what she looked like. Back to the business at hand. Another beer, another dancer, and then off to the store.

Back then I didn't know that lots of stores stayed open really late. Not that it wouldn't have mattered anyway. I didn't know that I could have staggered into some place at around eleven and found what I needed to wear, that is if I had any money left and knew what I wanted. I probably never intended to buy clothes that day, though certainly on my way out of the bank, through its revolving door, happy that I got to smile at my favorite teller, a Jamaican woman who had both ears pierced twice, but often only wore earrings in one ear, two large red tears that morning, I thought that I was on my way to buying clothes and getting a job.

The job offer: Teaching college freshmen how to write sentences and, if they got that far, compositions. The bottom of the educational barrel is crammed with fish you don't want to shoot or bruise because each of them represents money for a college's coffers.

The real job: Putting more money in a school's bank account so they will thank you and throw you a few scraps. I suppose the difference between a hunting dog and me was that the four-legged worker knew how to carry his prey back to the master, while I was supposed to convince the students that one day, because of this class, they would all be able to leap gracefully from their crummy little barrels to big fancy models, ones that looked like new cars and freshly painted apartments on nice streets somewhere. I was supposed to convince a classroom full of faces, the eager, the sullen, and the blank, that I was a locksmith who could help them open any door.

The assignment: Describe what it was like to make love on your parents' plastic covered couch. If you were allowed to kill someone, who would it be? If you ever used the word spic, kike, chink, faggot, nigger, wop, bitch, please explain in a three-paragraph essay what this word means to you.

Yes, Professor Schooner, I understand this job has a lot of responsibility. Yes, I understand what the word, responsibility, means. Yes, I realize that I am their only gateway to the future, that I am what stands between them and success, and that I must help them reach their goals.

The future: a shot of bourbon straight up and a cold beer in a frosted glass. Thanks, how much do I owe you?

I must have been trying to see China through the bottom of my dirty glass because I didn't realize Miss Pony Tail had slid onto the stool beside me.

"What are you drinking?"

"Bourbon and beer."

"My name's Lisa."

"Glad to meet you,"

"You have a name."

"Yeah, I think so. I'm not sure. Call me Doc, all my friends call me Bill."

Lisa laughs. "You know what I was doing, I was making a call because I wanted to get high. You know what I mean?"

"Yeah, I know what you mean. I do it every chance I get."

What Lisa meant was heroin. I thought she meant something else: marijuana, hash, maybe opium. For some reason, I was thinking of the medicinal opium I once had. Maybe because it was the same color as the cabbage and confetti carpet. A friend of mine mailed me some. It looked like a red clay cigar. I was wishing I had some more. Or I just didn't care. She said "high" and I said "yeah." That was enough. Who needs to know how to write a sentence?

"But I need some money and I gotta take a cab. Do you like me? You're sweet. We could both get high. It'll only cost thirty dollars, plus the cab. Fine stuff, really fine stuff."

"Thirty dollars, plus cab. Suppose I give you fifteen, pay for the cab. I'll just go with you," I say, as if I were escorting someone to the hospital so they can visit a friend.

"You don't want some." Lisa is incredulous. "You sure you don't want some?"

"Well, maybe. Who knows?," I answer, shrugging my shoulders.

By now I realize that I haven't quite translated what Lisa is talking about.

It sounds like, it looks like. Surprise, you wake up in a stainless steel chamber and realize that you've just reached the last chapter of your future. Gee, sir, but that was kind of quick. Can I go back and try again? No, not this time. Good luck, here, spin the big wheel. Oh dear, in ten years you get to come back as a three-legged kangaroo or maybe, if you're really lucky, an albino newt. Meanwhile, we'll just spend a little time together in here and get to know each other real well.

"Where did you say we were going?" I ask, knowing it didn't matter, knowing the only answer that would have surprised me was if Lisa had said, a clothing store. Given that we were just in a topless bar, I doubt she was inspired to buy a new wardrobe.

Lisa and I are in the cab, snuggling. It's dark out. Shit, I think to myself, I bet the stores are closed. How did it get so late so quick? Shit, my girlfriend's probably wondering where I am. I ought to call her. You can't call from a cab, stupid. Besides, what are you going to say? Oh, hi honey. I'm in a cab with this young woman who has just put my hand inside her blouse and licked her lips. Funny, she's not wearing lipstick. I didn't notice that before. Oh honey, don't worry, I'm too drunk to do anything but grope her.

Somehow we get there and, as promised, I pay the cabby. Lisa leads the way. We're walking down a dark street with no streetlights, they're all busted, on the Lower East Side, somewhere around Avenue C. Lisa is a homing pigeon and heads straight for a building with no lights and no windows, all boarded up except for this one hole punched in through the cement blocks that have been used to fill the doorway and first floor windows. These are serious, industrious little fuckers, I realize, and I'm about to meet them.

"Hey Ramon."

Lisa is halfway through the hole. I'm looking at the pleated red skirt riding up her legs, looking at her legs, short but shapely, well muscled, topped by a black garter belt. I didn't expect to see that there and I'm thinking: Gee, she's going to get her skirt dirty or tear her nylons if she climbs all the way in, which she does when she hears a whistle and an all-clear from a voice perched high above her, in the shadows.

I'm standing there, looking at the hole when Lisa puts her arm back through it and waggles her fingers.

"It's okay. Ramon's already here. C'mon."

We climb three eerily lit flights of stairs. There are cheap metal lamps suspended by thickly insulated orange wires hanging down from one of the bannisters on the upper floors. I realize there's water trickling down the walls. Had it been raining when I was in the bar? It's as if we were in a cave somewhere out in Nevada, above the high desert plain, two prospectors digging for gold.

We get to the third floor and, like moths, head for the light at the end of the hall. I begin slowing down, letting Lisa take the lead.

Ramon and another man, who never said his name, are waiting in the room, like priests ready to guide us to the electric chair. There's one lamp facing the wall and four devotional candles, the kind you can get in any supermarket or bodega, on a table, along with a metal spoon and two hypodermics. Two gouged wooden chairs. An old lumpy mattress is pressed up against the far wall, by a boarded-up window. Gray sheet and khaki green army blanket. No pillow.

On the walls our shadows are rising and falling, like Balinese puppets rowing away from some hideous sea creature. I listen hard, but I can't quite hear what the storyteller is saying.

I give Ramon fifteen dollars. That's the deal Lisa and I made in the cab. It was after I said I'd give her the money that she began unbuttoning her blouse. I saw a mole above her pale right breast with white lace, almost like a doily, decorating the top of her pink satin bra.

Lisa was a secretary who wore frilly underwear, as well as a junkie with a habit. This was something I was just beginning to learn. There's no such thing as mutually exclusive personalities. Everybody was more than one.

"What about you?" Ramon asks nonchalantly. "Aren't you going to join the party?"

I try to act equally nonchalant.

"No, not tonight," I answer, shrugging my shoulders, as if it were my loss rather than Ramon's.

"Oh, you're a weekend shooter."

Whew. Yes, that's what I am, a weekend shooter. I'll know what to say the next time I'm standing on the third floor of an abandoned building on the Lower East Side, talking to a dealer with eyes that are like black, bottomless holes.

"Yeah, you know how it is," which was my way of

saying, I think that's what I was doing, I had a job during the week. I didn't of course, but I wasn't going to tell Ramon that I had lots of time on my hands, that after tonight I wasn't even sure where I would be living, and that I still had more than fifty dollars in my pocket. No way.

I sensed that it was okay, that they weren't going to make me roll up my sleeves and prove to them that I was a weekend junkie. Ramon and his silent companion didn't suspect that I was an undercover cop. Besides, in the mid '70's in New York, the idea of a long-haired Chinese undercover cop busting dealers and junkies was just too preposterous to even begin considering. There are fairytales and there are fairytales.

Yes, along with a sports jacket, tie, shirt, and shoes, I had thought about going to a barber shop that afternoon, something I hadn't done since I was fourteen. It was going to be a big day. I was going to join the human race. But standing there in a dimly lit room, watching a woman, who was in her mid-twenties, tying a belt around her arm, I knew that I had decided to postpone this decision a little while longer. It was too big a jump, too rash an impulse to have followed all the way through. I wanted to stay where I was a little longer.

Ramon looked at Lisa shooting up and then at me, who was standing beside her, and, I swear, he winked.

Did we stand on one of the dark landings afterwards and kiss? Did she try to unzip my pants? Did I push her against the wall and begin pulling up her skirt? No. I was glad to be walking down the stairs, glad to be climbing out of the cave, and standing on a empty, dark street, breathing the dirty night air.

Somehow that night we found a cab that took us out of there, back to The Doll Pit. After my girlfriend and I broke up, I used to go there all the time, usually around midnight. I would sit at the bar with the waiters who had just gotten off their jobs in Chinatown, most of them still in uniform: white shirts, black pants, white socks, black shoes. A checkerboard. The cooks and dishwashers didn't bother to change. A black room full of men in stained white uniforms, kind of like a hospital or abattoir.

I used to think that I might get to see the waiters and cooks slumped down in their chairs, jerking off into their white hats. But that only happened after midnight in the Pagoda Palace, a movie theater right across from where my girlfriend and I lived. They showed porno flicks from Hong Kong, with subtitles in English and French should you want to follow the plot.

We, my girlfriend and I, went there a couple of times. We learned it was better not to sit too close to anyone else. People who go to porno flicks after midnight have an invisible wall around them and it's best not to get too close to the wall, much less its inhabitant. I know, because I've been on both sides of that wall.

Yes, Lisa and I went back to the bar where we first met, and I had another drink or two. She leaned on my arm, drowsily batted her eyelashes and asked me what time I was getting up. She told me she had to get up in the morning and go to work.

"Do you have an alarm clock? I need an alarm clock. My boss will kill me if I go to work late one more morning."

"No, I don't have an alarm clock. Sorry."

I was lying, of course. Everyone has an alarm clock.

Well, my girlfriend had an alarm clock, that's true. It was one of the things she unpacked when we moved in together. But I wasn't about to go back there and ask her if I could borrow it for my friend, Lisa. Besides, my interview wasn't until three, and I didn't want to get up in the morning.

You see, I did know a few things back then. I knew Lisa was a junkie who needed an alarm clock, that I was a guy who didn't know how to buy a sports jacket, and that we weren't a match made in heaven.

Sand

You know, I didn't want to go out and meet you somewhere in public. And I certainly didn't want you to come over here either. Not now and not like this, I didn't. Look at you. I don't know why I ever called you. I had to, I suppose. Yes, I had to, I had to find out if you're the monster I think you are. Can you show me that you're not a monster. Can you do that? Just this once. But you are a monster, aren't you? You can't help yourself. It's in your blood, your soul. Can you show me that you're not a monster? Can you prove I'm wrong? Can you do that? Can you prove that I don't know what I'm talking about? No, you couldn't prove it if you wanted to. Besides, I can see through all your little tricks. So don't try any on me. Got that? Don't try one of your pathetic little tricks on me. It might have worked yesterday, but today's another story. Yes, another story, thank you very much.

Just because people compliment you doesn't mean that you're much of anything. I've seen your ugly side, your mean, puny side. I've had you in my mouth, and heard you beg for more. Other people might look up to you, think you're some kind of giant or something. To me, you're just a worm that crawled into my bed one rainy night, and I didn't have the heart to throw you out.

It's nearly noon and a man and a woman are lying in a king-sized bed in a dark hotel suite. The sheet is pulled up to their chins, the thick velvet drapes and lace curtains are drawn, and the air conditioner is purring steadily. They are lying on their backs, side by side, staring at the ceiling, as if they're either in a morgue waiting to be examined or about to be shot into outer space. Neither of them has spoken to each other, though it's clear that both are awake and have been for some time. A maid knocks on the door. Which one of them do you think answers? What do you mean this is a trick question? Now why would I ask you a trick question? No, it's not something I read in a magazine. It's something I understood today, something important about us. All you have to do is tell me which one of them said something to the maid. And what did that person say?

I want you to bring two long green silk scarves, a pair of blue mittens, preferably a child's, and a very ripe, pink grapefruit. I want to play House.

The red leather interior is snug, and both of them liked to pretend they were in a sports car, something that could go faster than the all the other cars on the road. The man is driving. The woman beside him has pulled her skirt up, and placed her hands between her legs. The man speaks first. I've wanted to tell you something for a long time, something that I think needs to be said. But perhaps now is not the right moment. The woman smiles. What's the right moment? Well, I can see that we've reached an impasse, he says softly but sharply, and that you're going to continue playing games with me. This isn't a game, she whispers, because if it was, one of us would lose. And honey, it wouldn't be me.

One of them says to the other you know why I liked you? It was because you were soft in bed. The other one looks up, and, mishearing what has just been said, begins laughing. Yes, I am a little bit demented, but not so much as I thought you would notice.

I didn't know what he wanted, but I trusted him. And since then I haven't been able to trust anyone. You're the first. You know that, don't you? You're the first person I've trusted since then. Of course, I'm over it. You must know that by now. Look at all we've done together, all we've been through. See, my hands aren't even trembling. Here. Put your hands here. That's better.

Well, to tell you the honest truth. It was like he turned around and kicked me right in the heart, she says to her friend, tears filling her eyes, yes, right here in my heart. She stops. Hey, am I starting to sound like one of those country and western singers? Well if I am, that's too damned bad. Because what I feel is a real deep pain, and it's burning a hole in my heart. You do know what I'm getting at, don't you?

A smile begins to spread over her friend's face, like butter in a warm pan. Yes, the friend answers, nodding, her hands covering her face, I know what you mean.

Well, you want to know what I think, she says, smiling. I think your entire body reeks of decay. Yep, good old down to earth rotten to the core decay. The kind you are not going to find in either a candy store or a graveyard, but the kind that makes a dog's tongue drag along the ground.

They are waiting for someone to bring them a menu. It's the first time they've been alone in a restaurant in months. It's the business we're in, she tells him. We need to have dinner with other people. We need to do these things if we're going to get anywhere, you know that. We have to go out to dinner and we have to be seen. Luckily, most of them aren't boring. Anyway, now we're together and we're alone. She smiles at him, and then peeks quickly into the menu, like an eager child. You know, if you ever left me, I would die, she whispers. I would just curl up and die.

She picks up the phone. He had called her right when he said he would. She is lying on the couch, the phone pressed close to her ear. Tell me everything, she whispers. Everything down to the last, little detail. Don't leave anything out. I want to know every smell, every texture and color. I want to know what you tasted and what it tasted like. And then, when you hang up, come over here. I'll be ready.

It's not what you say exactly or even what you do, that's not what's bothering me. It's that there are different sides of you that don't seem to go together. Or shouldn't, anyway. I don't know how else to put it. You're the kind of puzzle I don't like and never have. The kind that leaves me feeling like I should have stayed home and watched TV or picked up a different book.

In one day he sees three women with whom he had once been involved. All of them are pregnant. All of them smile and wave when they see him. He wonders why all of them feel the need to nod and point discreetly at their stomachs.

Of course I meant what I said. Why would I've said it if I hadn't meant it? Sure, I've said things I didn't mean. Everyone does. But in this case, yes, I meant what I said. And no, I won't take it back, or change my mind, or anything else for that matter. Is that clear? Or should I say what I said again? Just in case you didn't hear me the first time.

Not once in the three years they were lovers did they sleep in each other's bed. Later, each of them wonders if this is the real reason their relationship lasted as long as it did, far longer than any other they've had, or is it what finally drove them apart, made them distrust each other and themselves?

He gets a letter from a woman who tells him she is about to get married. Although both men have the same name, she now realizes that she wants to marry only one of them.

After reading her letter, he sends her a note congratulating her for making the right decision. He doesn't know if it is the right decision, but he's glad that she didn't want to marry him.

I wanted to make you happy. I did. I just didn't know how. And neither did you. You didn't know how to make yourself happy. You didn't even know what happy meant. You kept telling me it was the name of somebody's wife, someone with lots of money. You said he had had a heart attack while making love to a young woman. You thought it was funny. And you told me this story over and over. But you weren't happy then and you're not happy now. Funny maybe, happy definitely not.

Topless

It's a quiet Sunday afternoon at Mike's Last Dive, and a few of the regulars are hanging around, drinking and passing the time. Like the others sitting at the bar, I'm half-watching the game when a woman taps me on the shoulder. She tells me her name is Serena and that she met me nearly ten years ago. I don't remember her, but I know she's telling me the truth when she begins describing the contraption I was in at the time.

One of my strongest memories of that day, she tells me, was when you started looking like a cherry popsicle wrapper. It was because of the late afternoon light coming in through the window. I think it was in the fall, late September or maybe early October, that I met you.

I don't know if I really looked like that, but I did feel like I had been crumpled up, and that no amount of ironing was ever going to straighten out my seams again. Maybe that's what makes Saints glow. Being crumpled up inside.

I motion to the empty stool next to me, but she doesn't seem in any hurry to take it, preferring instead to stand close beside me and tell me that she and Jimmy had thumbed a bunch of rides down to see me, spent a few hours hanging around my hospital room, and then went out to the highway and hitched home. The leaves had just started turning yellow and red. They didn't get back until way after midnight; and her mother was really angry because she wanted the family to get up early for church the next morning. She was still in high school, and Jimmy was the only kid from the town who had gone away to college. Back then, she says wistfully, I would have gone anywhere with him.

The room where Serena first met me had pale blue walls and a big window overlooking a parking lot. In one corner, suspended from the ceiling, was a television you rented by the day. There was always a pitcher of ice water and a plastic glass with a flexible straw within reach; and in the cabinet beside the bed there was a stainless steel bedpan that always felt as if it had just been taken out of the freezer. There were two beds. I was in the bed by the window, the bed that looked like a jungle gym.

I was remembering events and routines I had tried to forget about for years. For once, they didn't make me wince.

Every other Sunday we got roast beef, mashed potatoes, and string beans. A lump of chocolate pudding that looked like a prank you'd find in your neighborhood joke shop.

My favorite dessert was the petrified lemon cake, which I'm sure must have sat on some school cafeteria counter for at least a week before a well-meaning soul thought it would be nice if she donated the once crumbly little yellow slab, as well as all its unwanted brothers and sisters, to the local hospital. If charity begins at home, I'm sure glad I didn't grow up in that woman's house. Who knows what she would have cooked for dinner?

Pot roast, chicken pot pie, baked haddock, spaghetti with meat sauce, macaroni and cheese, turkey and stuffing—

meals my mother never learned to cook. These were the seven basic meals the hospital dietitian deemed necessary to a patient's full recovery, the axis of eating around which our world turned. Among the satellite meals were franks and beans, roast chicken, and stuffed sole. Knowing this was my diet, the nurses cheerfully brought me a large glass of prune juice promptly at seven every morning.

I didn't have to hear Serena's story to remember that room. Forty-four roommates came and left, while I mostly just lay there from one night in the spring of one year until one morning a few weeks after the beginning of the next. I've left apartments I rented sooner than that.

"Yeah, that was me all right. I was in double traction. Two broken legs; one femur, two tibias, and a fractured pelvis. I had brought a myriad of afflictions upon myself with a mixture of large quantities of vodka, marijuana, and the gas pedal of bad timing, but managed to suffer no major internal injuries. Except of course my broken bones. All those wires, weights, and pins you saw. They were needed just to hold my bones together. You want to know who I really am? Why I'm the first cousin of both Frankenstein and Humpty Dumpty."

I look at Serena and smile, like a salesman who's relieved, because the customer knows she's being handed one whopper of a line. "Personally," I tell her in my most theatrical whisper, "I felt like a turkey trussed up for Thanksgiving. Too bad you missed seeing me when I looked like I had just crawled out of a meat grinder."

Serena laughs, and it feels really good to hear someone laughing about my accident. I laugh too and go on, cheerful as a slightly inebriated Santa Claus reading some kid's wild wish list.

"Yep, that's what happens when you get drunk and try to do a cartwheel through the windshield of a car that's doing eighty until a tree jumps in the way. In all his excitement over this unexpected miracle of nature, Harry, that's the guy who was driving, neglected to tell me that he thought it would be prudent if we came to a sudden stop."

Serena is smiling. I see immediately that she has bright white teeth, like those you see in a TV commercial. "You know, you seemed kind of sad back then. That's what I said to Jimmy when we were on our way home."

"Sad? No, I wasn't sad. I had a nice clean place to sleep, a television, three square meals a day, and lots of time to read and daydream. Besides, I knew I never would be drafted, that the army would have to reclassify me as 4F. The army didn't want men with metal plates in their legs and pins holding their hips together. Seems they were afraid the screws would come loose at an inopportune moment. You might say they didn't want a loose screw with loose screws."

I stop and look at Serena, the halo of late afternoon light sparkling around her cascading black hair, its hints of purple and red. I nearly stop breathing because I can smell her, she's standing so close.

I don't really want to talk anymore about being in the hospital, because I know there is not much more I can laugh at, that I have reached the end of my monologue, and that once again I'm close to tripping over what I've always suspected is the real reason for the accident, which is three adolescents who drink one night because they are afraid of what will happen after they graduate or drop out. But it's too late. Like the tree that walked out of the woods, Serena had jumped into whatever road I was cruising down while I was watching a baseball game and daydreaming. This time, however, the impact was going to be softer, though still painful.

"My friends brought me lots of books. The doctor even said it was okay to have an occasional drink. He thought I was a drug addict, because I seemed to like the morphine they gave me those first couple of weeks. Boy, was he relieved to learn that I wasn't a junky. I nearly forgot about the war for those nine months. Well except when I watched television or had to send a letter to the draft board telling them that I couldn't report for my physical. I did say where they could find me and, if they were willing to pay for my shipping and return, that I would be more than happy to show up on the appointed day." I want to laugh, but I can't, so I look at Serena and shrug.

Serena looks at me thoughtfully for a moment with her large dark eyes. "You mean you don't daydream now."

"Of course I do. What do you think I'm doing here," I say blithely, glad that we had found another subject.

"Drinking."

Serena's right. It's Sunday afternoon and I'm drinking in Mike's Last Dive, a large square room with a pool table in the middle. I've been here all afternoon, though I'm not exactly mowing them down. It's just that I have nowhere else to go, nothing to do. I'm killing time.

You see, I'm no John Wayne when it comes to drinking, at least not on Sunday. Maybe Wayne Newton tippling slow and easy in Las Vegas, but not John Wayne needing to quench a big thirst. I usually only need to quench my thirst late at night, when the bartender is about to announce it's last call and my head is still clear and I can still walk in a straight line. I don't like to walk in a straight line after midnight, because it means you know where you're going, and I don't want to know where I'm going then because it isn't anyplace I want to be going to.

Finally, I manage to say it out loud. "Would you like to sit down?"

"You don't mind, do you?"

"No, please do. It would make me very happy. You know," I begin to lie even though there's no reason to, "I'm glad you said hello, because I haven't thought about all the months I was in the hospital in a long time, and no one I know here in New York knew me then. Do you know what I'm saying?"

"Sure I do. I grew up in the same small town as Jimmy. No one I've met here has ever heard of it, much less been there. Kind of weird. It's like the town I grew up in never existed. I might as well have been born in the Twilight Zone."

"Welcome to New York. What are you drinking? Why don't you try a Manhattan?" I say, as I try to get the bartender's attention and order two drinks.

A few hours and a few drinks later, Serena and I are walking up the West Side Highway, beside the oily, black Hudson River, heading north. She's pushing her bicycle and I'm beside her, slightly buzzed, but still able to walk in a fairly straight line or at least not bump into her. For once I'm glad I'm not drunk. We reach Canal Street and she begins turning to the right. I slow down, not sure what I'm going to do.

"I live in Soho, near Houston Street," Serena says matter-of-factly.

"Oh, I live a few blocks away in Little Italy," I say, relieved that we live near each other and that my walking with her is now a matter of necessity, rather than part of some plan. I'm glad the decision is taken out of my hands, because I wasn't sure what I wanted to do or say when it came time for us to go our separate ways.

How often does a woman come up to you in a bar and say she remembers meeting you in the hospital ten years ago? It makes me both happy and sad to go back in time and start remembering what it was like to spend months lying in bed, staring at a parking lot and the sky changing and not changing overhead. I watched TV, read lots of books, kept a journal I couldn't throw away after I left, but couldn't read either, and made up blissful little stories, though I remember none of them now. It was me who had been in the accident and me who is remembering it now. And yet, it's as if I am talking about a completely different person, which is both true and false. The problem is that I can't always tell which is which. All I remember are disconnected chapters.

I look at Serena, who, a few minutes earlier, made it clear that she didn't need any help with her bike. Serena is someone who knows how to stand out in a crowd, make people take notice by throwing them slightly off balance. She is dressed in baggy pink satin shorts, an oversized faded purple t-shirt, red sneakers accentuated by red knee socks, and looks incredibly sexy—a cross between a tomboy and gymnast. She tells me she's a schizophrenic dancer.

"The past six Saturdays, I've been dancing in the Sculpture Garden of the Museum of Modern Art during the afternoons. I also dance in different bars around 42nd Street. You might say I entertain the out-of-towners during the day, and the bridge and tunnel crowd at night.

Serena pauses for a second, as if she's considering what she's about to say next.

"Well, it's all for art and money. So far I haven't met anyone who has seen me dance in both places, the museum and the topless bar, it's called The Body Shop, that's B-A-W-D-Y. Maybe you'll be the first on your block to see me struggle for art and then strip for money."

I'm too surprised by the boldness of Serena's remark to say more than, "Maybe." We walk on in silence.

Ten minutes later, neither of us having spoken during that time, Serena announces, "I live just down this street."

"Oh well, it's a nice night. Let me walk you all the way home and then I'll be on my way." Yes, I'm thinking, to another bar. Maybe The Red Star. Maybe it's time I try and become John Wayne.

Are you surprised it didn't turn out that way? Or that Serena invited me to come up to her loft? which she explained was also a large dance studio that she and Diana, her roommate, rented out to dancers and dance companies that needed rehearsal space. I was until later.

"Yeah, that way we keep our overhead down and still have a place where we can practice."

Serena stops before getting out her keys and looks at me.

"I should tell you something before we go up there. Diana is out right now, but she'll be coming back later on. I don't know when."

Later that night, lying alone in bed, bathed in stale alcohol sweat and pale moonlight, I figure Serena is just another one of those late night encounters that occasionally happens if you spend lots of time in bars, and that we wouldn't see each other again. This bothers me, because what she said to me has started glowing in my imagination like a radioactive nightlight. Maybe it's better that I left her place, I keep telling myself, because wanting to stay and having to leave began making me feel like I was back in the hospital.

The loft was almost as big as a basketball court, and we were sitting on a bunkbed which was pushed up against the wall at the far end.

"There are," Serena said, handing me a joint, "all kinds of dancers in this city. Most of them think there's a top to the pyramid, but they're wrong. It's a heap, just a big heap made up of lots of little heaps, all of us writhing around like snakes in a basket."

I nodded, and handed her back the joint. I hadn't been talking as much since we entered the loft, because I was too busy trying to take everything in.

Serena went on. "I'm lucky, because I have the kind of body that allows me to writhe anywhere I want, at a museum or in a bar." The joint floated slowly between us, like a wounded firefly dragging itself across a tightrope. "You see, all along I've known I probably won't get famous. I can do what someone tells me to do, but I have no imagination when it comes to doing something on my own. Except when I'm dancing topless. Even then, they think I'm more of a prop than a dancer, something they can play with inside their steamy little brains. But one thing is for sure, whatever happens here, I won't leave this city brokenhearted."

"That's a good attitude to have," I whispered, though I wasn't quite sure I knew what I meant.

"You bet it is," Serena whispered fiercely, her eyes closed.

I turned and just stared at her in the candlelit loft, our shadows rocking back and forth, like sailors quietly playing cards in a storm. I held onto the joint and didn't say another word because I didn't want to break the shell into which she had climbed. I just sat there on the edge of the bunkbed, looking long and hard, as if I were her lover and I was watching her sleep, surrounded by candles, their tiny fiery tongues licking the sweet, delicious air.

An oddly attractive woman comes up to you in a bar and starts a conversation based on an unlikely coincidence. A couple of hours later, the both of you walk to her place, a big empty loft with a bunkbed at one end, a round wooden table, four unmatching chairs, and lots of candles, all of which she lights. This is what happened, how it began.

We slouched on the bunkbed, like kids in camp on a rainy day, and told each other stories. After smoking a joint and talking some more, we kissed each other goodnight and I went home, without her phone number, but knowing where she lived. Perhaps it should have ended there, a pleasant interlude. But it didn't. It seldom does.

A few months later, while walking back to my apartment one afternoon, I see Serena carrying a familiar, blue wooden chair into a building. A red one, its distant cousin, is sitting on the sidewalk. She doesn't see me so I wait for her to come out.

When Serena sees me, she looks more bemused than surprised.

"Hey Serena, what are you doing?"

"Oh hi, I'm moving in here. Diana and I got tired of trying to keep the loft going so we decided to split."

"Oh, that's too bad."

"No, it's not."

"Can I help?"

"No, I've just got this one thing to bring up, then

I'm done. Hey, if you're not doing anything, why don't you come by later on? Say around four, that's when I get home from work. I'm dancing in a better place these days, rich dermatologists in blue pinstripe suits. They like to see if they can find where I'm hiding my acne. Ugh." Serena scrunches up her face.

"Four," I repeat.

"Don't tell me you're asleep by then. Look at you. It's nearly two and you look like you just got up. Am I right?" Serena says, poking me playfully in the ribs. "Take a nap, if you need to."

"Okay," I say, meaning I'll take a nap and I'll come over.

Serena winks, turns around, and walks into the building, carrying the last chair.

I stand there, my heart racing. A few moments later, I hear my name and look up.

"I live on the second floor. 2 FE, if you get here after four. Don't worry about waking me. I have much too much energy when I come home to even begin thinking about going to sleep."

I know Serena's inviting me to spend the night with her, and I decide on the spot to come back at four that morning. I'm pretty sure that this time that I won't feel like I'm back in the hospital.

A rug dealer and an elevator operator, a lawyer and a school principal, a druggist and a word processor, a circus clown and a dietician, a bus driver and a gardener. Every couple has a routine, it is part of what holds them together. This is how Serena and I began ours.

After a few weeks we have it down smoother than

any train schedule. I usually leave The Red Star shortly before four and walk over to her apartment, where I sit on the stoop and wait for her cab to pull up. She wanted to give me the key, but I told her I'd rather wait, that I liked watching her get out of the cab, and I did, because I never knew what she would be wearing. A black baseball hat and satin jacket with the sleeves ripped off, shiny purple high heels and blue gym shorts. A chintzy black velvet evening gown and red sneakers. Serena seemed to have a whole wardrobe of exquisitely mismatched clothes. I was sure nothing went with anything else until she put them on.

It is still summer so most nights we sit outside and talk for a while before going in. Then we go up to her apartment and take a bath together. The bathtub is in the kitchen, which is really just a corner of her one-room studio. We sit there, in a room full of blazing candles, and Serena describes some of her customers and what they said to her.

"Yeah, I told him the last guy that handed me that line got burned where the sun don't shine. Got ten dollars and no hassle after I said that."

Batting her eyelashes, she'd go on, "You know, every night, one of them says he wants to marry me. Beats me why they think I'd be interested in marrying a man who sweats in an air conditioned topless bar. Me, I'm covered with goose bumps. It's like I got hives or something. And all those men staring up at me, as if they expect a miracle. What they don't understand is that I'm in control, not them. They want me to do something special for them. But I'm not doing anything for them, I'm doing it for me."

I sit there listening, my head propped against the rim of the tub. Sometimes Serena shakes me, making sure I haven't started drifting off, which I haven't. By the time we dry off and head for bed, the sun is turning the sky from a deep, rich blue to a milky blue, and, a few blocks away, the second wave of trucks is starting through the streets, going from Brooklyn to New Jersey.

Our routine is based on Serena's schedule. She usually makes a couple of hundred in tips on the nights she dances, and that is more than enough for her. Occasionally I sand floors and renovate lofts like the one she and Diana used to share, help make them into fancy digs for the lawyers and doctors who are moving into Soho in a steady but slow stream, like army ants migrating north. We have money, but don't spend much. A movie every few weeks or dinner in Chinatown, that's enough.

We don't need to buy drugs because Serena's customers keep giving her stuff, most of which she doesn't like and gives to me, and which I end up giving to my friends. I work when I have to, spend my days reading and writing, my nights hanging out in bars, waiting for Serena's cab to glide to a stop, see what costume she'll be wearing when she emerges, the cab driver looking at her as she walks away. During the day, she goes to her exercise class, auditions, or hangs out with her friends. I never meet hers, and she never meets mine.

One night, while we are sitting in the bathtub, the water still warm, Serena nudges my elbow with her foot. "Remember when I told you that I met you in the hospital?"

"Yeah, how could I forget."

"And that I had gone there with my friend, Jimmy, who had been in the backseat when it happened."

"Yeah, I've always wondered what happened to Jimmy. I heard he ended up in a mental hospital somewhere in Texas, right?"

"Houston. It was in Houston."

"Right, Houston. Something about a snake."

"You don't know the whole story?" Serena says, suddenly sitting up in the tub.

"No, not really. Someone, maybe Henry, wrote me a letter, but I couldn't tell if it was something he made up or not. We're always trying to fool each other, see if we could pull off a tall tale."

"Oh your friend didn't make it up. He didn't have to. You see, after Jimmy dropped out of school, he drifted around some and then, I don't know how, he managed to get a job as an assistant cook in a fancy restaurant in some highbrow Houston hotel. One of their gimmicks was to offer rattlesnake as an appetizer on the menu. The management said it tasted like wild desert chicken. Of course, that's what they say about frog's legs. They taste like succulent swamp chicken. In Florida, where I once danced for a month to make some money, I heard a waitress say that about alligator. They never say what the chicken tastes like, just that everything else tastes like chicken. Beats me. I guess they have to say it tastes like chicken. Be dumb if they said alligator tastes like alligator."

"Or skunk," I add. We both hold our noses and laugh. "Anyway, go on."

"Well, somehow Jimmy got hold of a defanged rattler from some medical laboratory and carried it into the restaurant one night. When no one was looking, he put it on a silver platter with one of those covers and sent it out into the dining room. The snake had a medal around its neck, like the kind you get if you're a hero. Well, the waiter bows before some fat, cigar-chomping Texan and his blonde beehive honeydew melon and ceremoniously lifts off the silver cover. You know, like in that movie with Bette Davis and

Joan Crawford. Anyway, everyone in the place just about shit because there's this rattlesnake inside, when it's supposed to be some kind of fancy roast or something. A drugged rattlesnake with a medal of some kind around its neck, and a note that says, Eat shit and fly."

We both laugh and begin splashing the water, like birds.

"So how did that get Jimmy into a mental hospital."

"I don't know, but it did. He used to write me from there. Said it was time he had to serve."

I'm not laughing anymore and neither is Serena. "Yeah, he wrote me a couple of times. I don't know if it was from the hospital, maybe. But then we stopped writing or maybe I stopped. I don't know." I'm looking down at the water when I say this because I don't want to look at Serena. I'm sure if we look at each other we'll start crying and be embarrassed that we are.

"That's what I was thinking about."

"About Jimmy?" I answer, knowing I'm wrong.

"No, not Jimmy. At least not about him being in the hospital. Just about me knowing him and him knowing you and now you and I being together," Serena said softly. "Maybe this was all meant to happen."

I sit up and look at Serena in the swaying candlelight, her black hair hanging down in long wet strands. She's hunched up, her head tilting forward, and her eyes are shut tight. I remember the first time she closed her eyes, but it isn't the same, and I'm not sure why.

"Let's go to bed," I say, interrupting whatever memory she is following.

"Yum, that sounds good."

A few nights later, while lying in bed, the light just starting to shift from deep black to indigo, Serena rolls over, props herself up on her elbows, and asks: "Do you think I'm like Jimmy?"

"Like Jimmy? What do you mean," I reply, as I begin fumbling around, looking for my cigarettes.

"A casualty. Jimmy once said he was a casualty. Do you think I'm a casualty."

I light my cigarette, because I want to put off saying anything for a few moments. Serena and I are lying next to each other, staring out the window, listening to the sounds of the city waking up. After a few minutes, I say softly, "I think we're all casualties in one way or another. Don't you?"

"I suppose so. A week ago I might have said no. But right now, I'm not sure. I'm not sure about much of anything. Hell, the other morning I was even thinking that I wanted to have a kid someday."

"Really."

"Uh-huh. Imagine that."

Every couple has a routine, which, like the weather, must change one day. They can't go on doing the same thing week after week, month after month, year after year. It just doesn't work that way. A freak storm, a delayed train, a flat tire, a broken arm, a bad dream, a war—something interrupts the pattern. Sometimes you don't want the routine to change, but other times you do.

I'm sitting in The Red Star and it's near closing time. In a few minutes I'll get up and head for the door. Serena lives a few blocks from here and my apartment is a few blocks from her place. I know what I'm going to do, but I don't know if I'll keep doing it. That's what Serena and I couldn't say to each other a few nights ago.

Who's better? The one who lies and everyone knows it? Or the one who doesn't even know when he's lying? Jimmy was right. What I'm wondering is how many times you have to end up in the hospital or sit dreaming in a topless bar before you can finally go home to an empty bed. And maybe when I know that, I'll know where I'm headed.

Hawaiian Cowboys

Even though the sun is already hot and bright, I'm walking briskly back to the house, because I'm in a hurry to tell my wife what Haraki said to me when I went to her general store to get some stuff for our drive around the island. Haraki didn't know, how could she? But she had made me very happy, happier than I've been in weeks.

Before I left for the store, my wife said to me: "Now, don't dawdle. You know how you like to dawdle in there, and it's going to take us around eight to ten hours to do this. There's one road we know we can't take because of the lava flow, and this other one cuts through the mountains and rain forest."

I was standing in the doorway, about to say something mundane to her, when she looked up from the map and continued: "Who knows how long it will take us if we go that way, probably hours judging by how many curves the road makes on the map. If you ask me, that road looks more crooked than a path you'd find in an ant nest."

My wife, who is a big believer in guide books and maps, is still looking at the map, which almost covers the kitchen table, when I come in. Without looking up, she asks: "Did you get everything?"

"You won't believe what just happened!"

"Really?"

"Haraki, you know, the old woman who owns the general store, just asked me what island I'm from. Isn't that great? She thinks I'm from here, from one of the other islands."

"So," my wife asks, "what did you say?"

I wasn't quite expecting this response, but I go on. "I told her I was from Manhattan."

"Yeah."

"Well, Haraki looked at me and began to sing, "Manhattan, Manhattan — Mickey Mantle, Roger Maris, and Jackie Robinson."

My wife doesn't say anything.

By this time, I'm exasperated because my wife doesn't seem to want to share my enthusiasm. "You know, she was wrong. Jackie didn't play in Manhattan, he played in Brooklyn, for the Dodgers."

"I thought the Dodgers played in Los Angeles."

We've already drifted into another rut, and there's no way back. "They didn't always," I say, knowing that the story I wanted to tell her had shattered into a bunch of details, none of which summed up what happened when I went to the store and Haraki asked if I was from Maui or Oahu.

For the past two weeks, Janet and I have been staying at her friend's house, which is on the main road of a little coffee-growing village perched, like a bird's nest, halfway up a mountain in Hawaii or, as everyone calls it, the Big Island.

Set back a few dozen yards from the road, the pink wooden house is near the edge of town, and next to a Japanese graveyard full of new black stones, old weathered gray obelisks, and vases of fresh cut flowers. The graveyard is a stage, and the ocean and sky are the backdrop. The stones face away from this world, toward the road and stone gateway and the people who can still see the world that surrounds them.

The house has a screened-in verandah and a large backyard, but you can't see the ocean, only a bit of it glistening through the wild fruit trees, their branches laden with ripening mangoes, papayas, and avocados. On either side of the yard are rows of thick banana trees separating the house from the graveyard and the rest of the village.

Janet's friend, Diane, is an investment banker who comes here for a month each winter. "It's my little hideaway," she told us over dinner a few days before we flew out here. "It's where I go to recover, as well as repair my tattered soul. Lord knows, I need to do that after playing with other people's money day in and day out."

Since we've been here we've done pretty much the same thing every day. We get up at dawn, and one of us, usually me, goes out in the backyard and picks some mangoes and papayas off the ground for breakfast. After that, I go to the general store and buy the local paper, which isn't all that local because it is flown in from Honolulu, while my wife brews a big pot of Kona coffee, toasts a few slices of sweet Portuguese bread, and washes and cuts the fruit.

After breakfast we pack a basket with our lunch, and get the rest of the items we'll need for our daily excursion: flippers, snorkeling masks, protective lotion, towels, bathing suits, sandals, sunglasses, and books.

Around eleven a.m. we get in the rented car and drive down the mountain to the beach, go snorkeling or lie in the

shade and read. Doze off, daydream—it's a life of pure indolence. Janet and I lie around, encouraging our minds to
wander.

The beach is a small stretch of white sand off a bumpy
dirt road that only a few people, none of them tourists, seem
to know about, and is usually deserted until the mid afternoon. Since we landed on this island, I've managed to finish
a dozen or so detective novels, while Janet has plowed her
way through thicker, more serious fare.

Diane's house has no television, no books, and only
one radio, which is in the kitchen. We sleep on the verandah overlooking the backyard full of fruit trees. The big four-
poster bed is safely nestled inside a gauzy mosquito net so
we usually sleep soundly until shortly before the sun begins
to peer above the horizon, spilling its soothing heat and
brightness across the ocean. During dinner, Diane had said
there were no birds left on the island, but she was wrong.
There's a bunch of them who are all too happy to get us
ready for the sun's debut.

After dinner, which is usually grilled ahi and fresh
avocados, Janet consults her guide book or lists the different
fish we sighted while snorkeling earlier in the day. I'm con-
tent to flip through the pages of another detective novel,
and wonder if I should go on when I know who's doing
the killing, but not necessarily why. Except for the plots,
the books are pretty much the same. All the detectives are
thin, scarred loners moving silently through the maze of a
terrified city. Before turning out the light on the verandah,
Janet and I count the geckos slithering up the columns and
across the ceiling.

A few days ago we got tired of going to the beach,
and decided to spend a day driving around the island. Maybe
indolence isn't all that it's cracked up to be. Maybe it's time

our bodies began wandering as well. When we were at the beach, we continued snorkeling and reading, but spent the next few mornings and evenings looking at maps and consulting the various guide books we had brought with us. Finally we figured we had studied enough to venture forth, to do something besides lie around in the sun.

We weren't really going to go all the way around the island, because that would take more than a day, and Janet figured it was both easier and more economical to come back here the same night. But we made up our minds that we weren't going to continue spending every day we were here lounging around on the beach. The plan was to cross through as many different kinds of landscapes as possible, to see some of the many distinct worlds and memorable phenomena contained on the island; hardened black lava beds, tropical rain forests, rugged beaches, oil tankers, grazing lands, and arid fields were on our list of places to visit.

The first part of the drive took us down the mountain and past both the airport and the dirt road to our beach. We were heading towards the other end of the island. Janet drove, while I stared out the window. It was a bright, cool day. "A perfect photo op," as Janet put it, before we climbed into the car.

"So far, I've counted eleven."

"Eleven? Are you sure?"

"Yep. Seems like they are doing a lot of moving around today. Must be that school is over and they're on vacation."

Janet and I both laugh.

"Kind of crazy, isn't it?"

"It sure is. I mean, what were they thinking?"

Janet and I had read in one of the guides that someone decided that bringing the mongoose to Hawaii would solve the rat problem. The rats had been stowaways on the ships that stopped here, but the mongoose was an invited guest. However, the mongoose importer had made a serious and irreversible miscalculation. The rat does its food-gathering at night, beneath the moon and stars, while the mongoose likes to do its hunting in broad daylight. The rat and the mongoose are not even, as Sinatra sings, strangers in the night.

Shortly after being let loose, the mongoose began growing fat and happy on a diet of brightly colored birds, which weren't prepared to deal with these nasty little creatures. Consequently, so Diane told us the night we all went out for sushi and a lesson on how her house worked, there are no birds on the island. Diane was exaggerating, of course, because like most people who stay on the island for a few weeks each year, she imagines that Hawaii was once a kind of perfect paradise, a peaceable kingdom where all creatures lived in radiant harmony. The fact is, on Hawaii, all the creatures, whether man, animal, or insect, came from somewhere else. Flora and fauna too. Everything floated, swam, flew, or was carried here from there, wherever there was.

When Gertrude Stein was in Oakland, she wrote: There is no there there. What if she had come to Hawaii? What would she have written then? There is only there there. This was something I kept mulling over, something I found comforting to remember. All of us are from different islands.

As I told Haraki, I was from Manhattan. Going to her store every day, looking around at the odd items on its dusty shelves, I had learned a little about Haraki, though not enough to satisfy my curiosity. Her parents and husband were buried in the graveyard, and all five of her children had moved to other islands or the mainland. They visited her on holidays, and that was enough for her. She had fourteen grandchildren, and none of them were Yankee or Dodger fans. I couldn't tell how old she was, and didn't feel it proper to ask. She had deep vertical lines in her face and a big, toothy smile, like a Halloween pumpkin that had been left out on the porch a couple of weeks too long.

"What're you thinking about now?" Janet asked.

"Oh nothing, the usual. You know. Daydreaming."

"Well, don't get morbid on me. We've only just started. We have at least another seven or eight hours to go."

"Don't worry. I'm not getting morbid."

"Well, the only reason I say that is because you seem different lately. It's like coming here has done something to you."

"Done something to me?" I ask.

"Yeah, done something to you. I mean, like you seem to think about everything for a long time, make it into something important. It's like you're cooking some kind of weird mental stew. Remember, when we were in Honolulu and the Japanese cab driver kept asking you why we hadn't gone to Pearl Harbor yet. He kept telling you that you should take me to Pearl Harbor before we left. And you got mad at him, though you didn't let him know how mad you were. But you were mad all right. Kept muttering about him all through dinner. I mean, sometimes it seems as if everything gets to you."

"Oh, but that was depressing."

"Depressing. What was depressing about it? He meant well."

"Don't you see? That's what was really depressing

about it. A Japanese man in his early sixties tells me that I should go to Pearl Harbor. For what? Does that mean he's more American or something? Does it mean that I'm not, because I haven't gone and don't intend to? What am I supposed to say? That I like going to the Bishop's Museum more, that I'd rather look at all the specimens of extinct birds, that I like looking at the feathered robes, that I like learning about who and what were here before any of us arrived."

Janet falls silent. I didn't mean to argue with her, but it's too late. After a few seconds of silence, she pushes the button for the radio. A classical music station. She pushes it again, and Mahler's Fifth Symphony is quickly replaced by what I imagine to be a slick-haired, open-shirted man hyperventilating about the "oldies but goodies we have in store for you."

The sky and ocean are different but complementary shades of bright blue. The beach and ocean are to our left, and the black lava beds are to our right. There are almost no other cars on the highway. The air-conditioned interior of the car is filled with music, the dj's well-oiled pitter-patter, and our silence. Each of us is remembering something we did or said when a particular golden oldie first hit the air-waves. Bob Dylan, Jimi Hendrix, Martha Wells, Buffalo Springfield, Screaming Jay Hawkins, and Diana Ross and the Supremes. We drift back and forth in time, while Janet keeps the car moving forward.

For the past hour we've been climbing slowly but steadily. The beaches and ocean have given way to a mountainous landscape that reminds me, in some odd way, of the afternoon I spent driving west, from El Paso into New Mexico, past White Sands. I'm not sure why, though I think it has something to do with the way the sky comes down to meet the curving road and the dry, mountainous terrain. It's as if the sky and wind ran their fingers through the earth, scraping and pushing dirt and rocks aside.

Before we started this part of the trip, we stopped at a roadside stand and ate lunch, which was an odd combination of Japanese and American food, all of which came in a lacquered wooden box, a bento box. I told Janet that this was the way lunch was served to the people who attended the theater in Japan, and that someone must have transplanted it here.

The box had little compartments full of pieces of fish and vegetable tempura, meat that was a mysterious and not altogether appetizing hybrid of fried pork and sweet bologna, rice wrapped in seaweed, and pickled cucumbers. Like the mongoose, it seemed both completely out of place and the perfect thing to serve at a rundown roadside stand, near a glassy harbor full of huge oil tankers waiting to offload their cargo into the silver storage tanks, glistening like sunbathers in the bright noon heat, a few hundred yards away from our shady picnic table.

When I was finished extolling the virtues of our lunch, Janet looked at me incredulously. "This has got to be one of the strangest meals I've ever eaten. I mean what is this thing here?" she asked.

"I must admit I don't know," I answered, "but that's not the point. In this case, it's the idea that counts and not the food."

We both managed to laugh, before getting up and dumping what we didn't eat in the trash and returning our boxes to the young man, who had had no other customers come in while we were eating.

"If you ask me, everyone in the town knows to

go somewhere else," Janet said once we were in the car.

"Yeah, well. I didn't say it was going to be good, I just said I knew where it came from."

"The idea maybe, but not the food. Ugh, fried Spam and raw fish. If you ask me, a bad idea leads to bad food."

I didn't disagree.

At the top of an incline, and knowing there are others ahead, Janet pulls the car off the road and we get out. We stand by the railing and look down at a few ramshackle houses that look empty and abandoned in the rolling, rocky fields of thick, yellowing shrubs and short, dry grass. Where did their inhabitants go once they left here? To another island? Back to the mainland? Or further out into the Pacific?

According to the guide book, in a few miles the weather will start to change, and the landscape that follows is suitable for grazing. There's a number of big cattle ranches located in this part of the island, and one ranch is listed as being among the largest in the United States.

Janet sits on a big rock, takes out her notebook, and makes a list of what we've seen. She ticks them off, as she writes quickly but methodically.

— The miles of black lava which seem to turn almost blue in the bright light. The white rocks that people use to spell out their names or affiliations. Fraternities and sororities. Jimmy loves Ellen. Bobby hates Jessica who loves the wrong boy. Sue and Max Forever or However Long it Takes. So Long To Mickey From All The Fiery Flagellators.

— The row of elegant white buildings by the beach, the electronic gate just off the road, and the modest but telling sign indicating a private resort, where, we learned from one of the guides, each party has their own chef and masseuse, and each house comes with a private swimming pool. We try and remember who we've heard has stayed there.

— A dusty, hot town for the multi-national crews of the oil tankers.

— Another town which caters to surfers, many of them from California.

— A dense, wet jungle full of shrieking birds.

— High waves pounding a jagged, rocky shore.

— Cacti behind a barbed wire fence, like sentinels or priests.

— Strange flowers, some of which we are able to recognize.

— Twenty-seven road kills.

I kept looking at the shacks, tilting and tumbling, glad that much of this had been documented on three rolls of film. We didn't take many pictures in Honolulu, but standing here, by the side of a dusty road, I think maybe we should have.

In Honolulu I kept looking at the couples, marveling at how many of them seemed, like Janet and me, to be made up of people from different races and cultures. At times I wondered why my parents didn't stop here, why they decided to continue on their trip to America, why they thought they should go to the mainland. They had sailed from China shortly after the end of World War II, and had stopped in Honolulu for a few days. Maybe the place was too rough for them back then, but I don't think so. They had been in China throughout the war so Hawaii should have seemed calm and peaceful to them. Maybe not paradise, but certainly better than the world they left behind.

Janet's ancestors came from the opposite direction, from England. As she liked to tell me, they weren't on the Mayflower because it was too expensive. They were thrifty people who decided to take a lesser-known ship because the tickets were cheaper. Janet was as proud of her heritage as I was confused about my Dutch father and Chinese mother. Maybe that's why I was ready to come to Hawaii. Janet wanted to relax, but I wanted something else, though I didn't know what. It wasn't detective novels, but being a detective. I was looking for answers, though I would probably be the last to admit it. So we decided that instead of going to Martha's Vineyard, which was what Janet and I usually did in the summer, and spending time with her parents, neither of whom I liked, we would take Diane up on her generous offer, and spend some time in Hawaii. We've been here nearly a month, and, for different reasons, each of us feels as if the place is tugging at us, asking us to stay.

We get back in the car and start driving. Within a few minutes the temperature begins getting noticeably cooler and the landscape changes abruptly from yellow to green. It's as if someone has pushed a button, and a new slide has dropped into the projector. I turn off the air conditioner and roll down my window. Janet does the same. There are lush fields on either side of the two-lane highway. The incline is slighter now, and we know we're about to reach a plateau, where the land flattens out beneath the sun. We may be a few thousand feet closer to the sun, but the weather here is cool and breezy. Springtime in Montana.

We pull over once more, get out, stretch our legs, look at the cattle grazing on the other side of the fence, and decide we will stop for something to drink in the town the map indicates is fairly close. By now I am sure that somewhere on this island is a painter who is recording all the colors and shades of light that one can find by simply walking outdoors. I know I'm not that person because I've just started to see this place, and cannot look at it hard enough to remember it all. Perhaps the tug I feel is similar to one that most people, who come here for the first time, have when they realize that they may never return once they leave. Perhaps, knowing I can't see it all, I've started to close my eyes a little.

Driving down the mountain this morning, Janet and I remembered what the woman on the radio said before we left the house. The lava flow had almost reached the highway on the south side of the island. Within a day or two the highway would be cut in half by the river of molten lava that was moving, like a huge red snake, toward the sea. The number of houses swallowed by the lava had climbed to seventeen. Another six houses were in danger. All through this litany of destruction the woman's voice was calm and unbroken as the sea. She was one of those people who knew that none of us are in control.

Hawaii is an island with an appetite. The ocean, volcanoes, and jungles are like hungry, angry infants. Perhaps this is what everyone who has lived here for a while knows, that they are only guests. I realize that Haraki has hardly ever mentioned the volcano when I've been in her store. It's not that she doesn't care. I'm sure she does, because she was friendly to me the very first time I went in there. No, it's something else that causes her to seldom speak about what is going on just a few miles from her village, something I'm not sure I understand.

I blink twice, the second time because I'm surprised by what I see. We've driven into a small town that looks like something you'd see in Wyoming or Texas, or maybe a movie of the west. We've entered cowboy country. There are stores selling fancy cowboy boots, western style shirts and belts, a large storeroom full of shiny Harley Davidsons, and a huge lot full of brand new pickup trucks. I spot a sign and point to a diner on the next block.

"Look, there's a place. I'm sure we can get something to drink there."

"Yeah, that looks good. I'll park right here."

We go in and sit down in a booth. Even though it is late in the afternoon, the place is nearly full. A lot of men are sitting at one big table, talking and gesturing. At another table, young men and women hang out, flirting and joking with each other. Some mothers have come in to relax and talk to their friends. Their children run around, making noises that no one seems to notice. A couple of older men, sitting alone at the counter, are eating pie and drinking coffee. I realize many of these people are eating dinner early, before the sun goes down, and that they aren't on vacation.

I feel like a nosy neighbor who wants to see who's living on the other side of the fence, what they're up to. Most of the men are dressed like cowboys, and almost all of them are Asian or Hawaiian. Chinese, Japanese, Filipino, Polynesian, and Samoan. They're all sizes and shapes. Some are thin and wiry, while two are as big and thick as stone fireplaces. I remember a photograph of me when I was a child, dressed up like Hopalong Cassidy, and the Davy Crockett hat I begged my mother to buy me for Christmas. This was before I realized I could never be Wyatt Earp, Jesse James, or Daniel Boone.

I look around and see men in fancy alligator boots, silver belts, and embroidered shirts. Others are in dusty dungarees, leather chaps, sweat stained shirts, and bandanas. None of them are pretending, like I was when I was a child.

100

Janet is reading the menu, while I'm looking at the customers, trying to hear what they're saying. I try to see what has been embroidered on their denim shirts, a bird-of-paradise flower or a hummingbird, perhaps. I imagine a black Hawaiian shirt with bright red flowers, like the one Georgia O'Keeffe painted when she was here, green cacti, saddles and horseshoes. Nature mixed with things that might have been brought here a hundred years ago, in the days when the West was still being won by some and lost by others. I feel dizzy and exhilarated, sad and uneasy.

Janet interrupts my reverie, "Do you know what you are going to get?"

"An iced tea."

"Hmm, that sounds good. I'll get one too."

Then, suddenly, I smile. "What kind of tea do you think it will be?"

"What do you mean?"

"You know, the iced tea. I'm just wondering if it will be American or Chinese, plain teabag or sweet jasmine, cowboy or instant, red zinger or honeyed essence of green hummingbird? I'm wondering if they give you those kinds of choices. If they don't, they ought to."

Janet looks me at me oddly, as if she is afraid that I might be slipping off into what she calls my morbid phase.

"Cowboy tea? Don't you mean coffee, cowboy coffee?"

"Yes, that's what I meant," I whisper, nodding and smiling, as if to reassure my wife that I'm not about to get moody on her, and that I now realize I've just told her a bad joke.

We close our menus and lean back against the red leather booth and smile awkwardly at each other. I'm not sure if these are real smiles or not, but I realize that somehow, maybe inevitably, Janet and I have become strangers. Perhaps it will pass, perhaps it won't. It's still too early to tell.

I look around once more, and decide I'll try and sit quietly and calmly, that I'll wait until the waitress brings us our order, before I start telling my wife that there are no lifeboats in Hawaii, that there are only islands within islands, and that it's nearly time for us to leave. We may be on an island that's growing bigger each day, but it's also sinking into the sea.

Heaven and Earth

The slightly balding, bespectacled figure of Il Maestro, Norman Rockwell, hovers at the edge of the scene, holding a #2 round brush. His flabby extremities are as milky gray and still as Michelangelo's David. It is a clear, dark summer night and the glistening black sky is dotted with stars.

Rockwell is standing in the middle of the block, beneath an amber spotlight, looking up and down the wide, empty street of a small New England town. It is quite apparent to him that something has happened to the world since he had to take leave of it. Something he cannot quite comprehend. For while the world looks very much the same, he is convinced the things and people inside it are very different from before. He blinks rapidly, thinking this will cause everything he remembers to fall back into place, like a contact lens.

Oh gods of disdain riding your chariots through the black, jeweled sky, Rockwell whispers, please tell me what has happened to the freckle-faced murderer I used to adore? Oh my puny gallivanter who once crawled into the mouth of a bottle, where have you hidden yourself? And what about the obese mayor who liked to stop and scratch his crotch before entering the sunlit courtroom, its worn wooden benches full of fluttering fans, each delicately painted with purple petunias and pink roses? Where are the rows of befuddled faces that droop like old Halloween candles? their parched mouths full of broken stumps? Where are the grimacers, gripers, and graspers? Where are the hooligans and hags?

Rockwell looks dazed, and his large, lined forehead glistens with sweat.

Oh yes, and what ever happened to the scrawny butcher no one trusted, because he looked like a wet scarecrow? And men stuffed with straw are not known to savor either the texture or flavor of meat. Where is the shovel-faced lady in the faded blue gingham dress, who used to clomp headlong down these hallowed halls, her yellow fangs trailing a kite string of spittle in the whirlwind of grit and dust that followed her everywhere, like a little spotted dog?

Rockwell stops for a second, and then goes on with his litany.

Where are the sullen ones I once celebrated, the broken ones I still love? I say it's a damned shame, but the world has turned into a pile of slimy oatmeal, a mountain of poodle ooze on a bright green lawn, a lice-infested thing tottering on the edge of a sulfurous volcano. The world's become a pestilence since I've left. A dark, rotted thing.

Suddenly, like Bela Lugosi's pallid, puffy Dracula, Norman Rockwell whirls around and strides purposefully back down Main Street, towards his recently renovated carriage house, its bedroom windows blazing with Christmas lights from Mexico, little elves with pointed caps riding red chili pepper sleds.

Meanwhile, unbeknownst to Rockwell, Eileen, his

second wife, an ex-gymnast and former airline stewardess with a now defunct Caribbean airline, is hiding in the darkened parlor, waiting for him to open the front door. Hearing her husband's footsteps as he quickly bounds up the stairs two at a time and crosses the porch, she feels her heavily-powdered throat beginning to constrict, as if he is once again tightening the grip around her neck with the blue and yellow fleur-de-lis silk scarf he bought at a duty-free shop during his last flight to Singapore. She remembers the first time her husband used it and how his eyes glinted, like diamonds, in the dark.

In her right hand is the shiny new remote control, which is, as the hooded salesman told her, capable of surprising even you with all the little things it can do. She remembers what her father said to her many years ago, as he lay sprawled on the floor: This is a world where anything can happen and it usually does. She begins to punch in the sequence that will satisfy the thirst caught in her throat.

Meanwhile, the freckle-faced young man is thinking that there are two views of this room, the one he is seeing and the one that is reflected in the window behind him. He has, of course, failed to recognize the third and even fourth view of the room he and his wife presently occupy.

I can look at one or the other, but not both at the same time. But if I were the window rather than the man sitting in this chair, then whatever my wife said or did would pass right through me. I would be a conduit between one world and another.

His wife is standing by the stove, occasionally bending over and stirring what is simmering in a large cast iron pot. On the wall behind her is a painting of a robin she bought at a flea market in Vermont, near Middlebury, two summers ago.

The freckle-faced man looks at the painting, rather than his wife, whose face is full of benign concentration as she stares into the pot and thinks about what else might be added to the bubbling green stew. When his wife brought the painting up to the man behind the counter, he looked her in the eyes and said, "I see you're a real lover of art. Well, this painting was done by one of those folks who turns to art, because he knows there is absolutely nothing else he can do. Art, they say, is a calling. Well, lemme tell you something, little lady, this here fellah was definitely called. Yes he was."

"If you ask me," his wife says, interrupting his revery, "you have no reason to be depressed. I mean, it didn't turn out exactly the way you wanted it to. Nothing does, you know. But still, it turned out better than it has for me. Now, in my case, yes my case," and she begins to laugh, though the reason for this is unclear to either of them.

The freckle-faced man is seated at a table, looking at the maroon and white contemporary Wedgewood plate she has set before him. It shows an English hunting scene: three robust men with muskets slung over their shoulders. They're walking jauntily into the woods, surrounded by nine or ten sleek springer spaniels. Thick, full trees on either side of the pebbled path. Young women and children in the foreground, all of them cheerfully waving good-bye. In the distance, a flock of small birds rises above the trees.

He is thinking that the dishes, as well as the wine glasses, silverware, and napkins, are parts of various sets that have been given to them by her family. They are things she has used before, in another life, and it is a life she refers to often, usually with a tinge of nostalgia.

"You," she says sweetly, "have no reason to complain."

"I wasn't complaining. I told you I was depressed. I know it's silly, but sometimes I can't help it," he replies, hoping this would be the end of it.

"Yeah," she says, her tone changing, "well, when something bad happens to me, I don't get like you. I don't sit around the house, staring at the walls like some kind of mental patient. Something bad happens to you and you go kerplunk. Like a frog jumping off the Empire State building because he has forgotten that it's not a lily pad."

She turns and looks at him. "For crying out loud, you're as sensitive as a leaf."

She laughs at her joke, then declaims, in a loud sing-song voice: "Oh my little green leaf, don't you know that your dear young wife ain't getting no relief."

"Will you stop?" he asks, his voice rising.

"What's with you anyway?" she says, as if she hasn't heard him or noticed that his voice is strained.

"I said, will you stop?" His voice is insistent.

"Yeah," she answers nonchalantly, lifting the wooden spoon to her lips, and then smacking them loudly together. "Oh slurping, burping good," she cheerfully announces, "this dinner is almost done."

Suddenly, she stops what she is doing and looks at him. "Let me just say this one more thing. I promise, this will be the last thing I say anything else about," she pauses, "your mood. Anyway, the next time something bad happens to you, I wish you wouldn't take it so seriously. It affects me too, you know."

"I did ask you to stop," he says to the plate, which

he has started to turn, around and around, as if it's a steering wheel that has come loose in his hands.

"What did you say?" she asks mockingly, her eyebrows arched.

"I asked you to stop. I asked you to fucking stop," he yells. And with that he brings his fist down onto the plate, breaking it neatly in half. "But you wouldn't. Twice, earlier tonight, I said, please stop. I said I was depressed. I said I was sorry. But did it matter? No, you just went on prattling away, like some kind of demented bird. Well, fuck you."

His wife looks at him, her arms folded across her chest, the wooden spoon held firmly in her right hand, and says nothing. It is the first time he has broken a dish, but she realizes that it will probably not be the last. She decides once again to act as if nothing unusual has passed between them, as if this is the way they always talk to each other.

The man gets up, grabs his leather jacket, and walks out, slamming the door behind him.

Where am I going to go? What am I going to do?

He leans in the doorway for a minute or two, tries to catch his breath, and then steps off the stoop and walks quickly down the street. After a few blocks he comes to an empty basketball court, which is surrounded by a high chain-link fence. There are three wooden benches, which face the street. Although all of them are empty, he decides to sit on the one that is furthest away from the streetlight and which is near a wall and under a tree. It is dark out and only a few other people are on the street.

Eventually the man no longer feels his heart hammering in his chest, like a frantic prisoner. He relaxes, stretches one arm along the back of the wooden bench.

How many times have I done this? he asks himself. He is thinking about the many arguments he's had with his former girlfriends and, now, his wife. The time he threw his typewriter down an airshaft. The broken picture frame. He had thrown a cup, thinking it would hit the wall, but, instead, it hit a drawing given to him by a friend's father. When he tried to pick the remaining pieces of glass out of the frame, one of them fell and stuck into his arm.

He rubs his arm, and thinks he feels the swollen scar beneath the soft leather sleeve of his coat.

Stop this. Just stop, he thinks.

He sits back, and once again stretches his arm along the top of the bench, just as he did when he first sat down. But he can't stop and he knows it.

After a few moments, he begins counting the things he has broken. He is sure this habit of counting started when he was a child, and his father unfurled his belt like a saber, raised it over his head, again and again.

No, he thinks to himself, it's me and the things I've broken. That other part of my life is over, done with. He stops, looks up, and sees a woman walking by. She's wearing a thin black raincoat, and her hands are thrust deep in its ample pockets, as if she might be holding onto something precious. She looks graceful and self-contained, even though she's in a hurry. But it's her long braid that really catches his attention, gray and brown and halfway down her back, carefully and lovingly knotted together like a soft rope. He leans forward and watches her as she crosses the wet street, its small puddles, with quick, long leaps, and goes into a noisy restaurant on the corner.

The freckle-faced man does not know how long he has been sitting there, maybe an hour. It is a cold, damp autumn night. The first time he and his wife had an argument, he got up and stormed out, because he had to take his rage outside, where it could expand without bumping into anything or anyone. Later, when he returned, his wife was asleep. It was as if the argument never happened.

This was not the first time he had walked out in the middle of something she was saying. It was, however, the first time he'd broken something. When will I stop counting up the things I have done wrong? When will I stop being like my father and keeping a ledger?

He had yelled at himself about this enough. And for a long time he had been sitting on the cold bench wondering why, when he had returned before, his wife always acted as if nothing had happened. It was as if the argument did take place only in his mind, the one, as she put it, of a mental patient. Well, he thinks, at least this time there's evidence.

Evidence. Why must there always be some kind of evidence? What evidence had his father left behind? What besides his memories? This is the question that he is always afraid to begin answering, because he is sure he is stuck inside his memories, and that there is no way of getting out.

His wife is working in her studio, at the far end of the loft, which is long and narrow, like a boxcar. Except for the lights in her studio and the single light shining above the dining room table, like the huge, glowing eye of Cyclops, the place is as dark as a mine. And, like ancient miners, each of whom is busy panning for gold, neither of them says anything to the other. The table is empty, as if no one recently sat down at it and began eating in silence.

110

The freckle-faced man finds it strange that he is hungry and wants something to eat. Opening the refrigerator, he sees a big bowl full of pieces of chicken covered in some kind of green sauce. The wine bottle has been opened. Another large bowl contains the glistening remains of a salad. He closes the refrigerator and walks over to the sink, which is empty, everything washed and stacked neatly in the wooden rack, and sees the broken dish rising from the trash, like two knives or wings.

As he stands there, his hands grasping the rim of the sink, he notices that the painting of the robin is no longer on the wall. He sneaks another glance at the trash, and, for one brief moment, realizes that he is disappointed not to see the painting pushed down into the stained, brown shopping bag, a mangled mess.

He looks back at the wall, the net white rectangle where the painting prevented any dust from settling, and remembers what else the man had said to his wife when she purchased the painting, "Art, you must understand, called out to him one winter night, and he answered the best way he knew how."

A sudden chill ripples through him, causing him to shudder, as if he is trying to shake loose a butterfly caught inside his shirt.

He leans back over the sink, rests his elbows on its stainless steel rim, and begins rubbing his left arm, not realizing that he still has on his jacket, and that the leather sleeve is soft, cool, and damp. Behind him, the glistening window allows the entire scene to pass unimpeded through its rain-washed rectangle so that if a person in the building across the street were to stand in his apartment and look out his window, he would see nothing he has not seen before. A man standing over the sink, lost in thought.

Meanwhile, inside the kitchen, the window reflects another view of the freckle-faced man, which is that of someone with his head bowed before a dust-streaked white wall, trying to imagine what it is like to be a child who has been taught to pray.

But he doesn't want to begin praying because he believes it is a form of screaming. And whoever answers prayers doesn't answer those who scream, this much he has learned. Instead, for some reason that he still doesn't quite understand, perhaps because he expected to see the painting of the bird above the sink, he begins remembering the magazines his parents used to buy, the pictures on the covers, and the stories he was too young to read inside.

Someone had painted the idyllic scenes on their glossy covers, someone whose name had become synonymous with innocence and goodness. He is thinking about these towns, streets, and rooms that never really existed. And, other than his wife, he is wondering if he has ever met anyone else who believes that they have sat on a bench in a town some call Paradise Corners, a shadowless place where, it is said, everyone sees through everyone else.

How to Become Chinese

I was taking a cab home. It was late, and the subways, trolleys, and buses had stopped running. The cab driver seemed suspicious and kept glancing at me in the rear view mirror. I thought it was because I had passed most of the night alone in a bar, drinking. Maybe he was worried that I had a gun and was planning to rob him. Or he thought I'd stiff him for the fare. What did he see? A leather-jacketed man slumped down in the corner, looking out his window, lost in thought. Maybe I was talking to myself. I've done that before and not even been aware of it. Certainly, I was close to being drunk.

We were hurtling down the empty streets, like a tin can with two marbles inside. When I shifted around because I wanted to get more comfortable, I not only realized that the traffic lights were rushing toward us, green and red dots glowing in the night, but I also noticed the driver's eyes kept peering out of the rearview mirror's silvery rectangle. Like someone inside a box, his eyes following you as you walk by. It made me even more nervous. Who was this guy? And why was he in such a hurry?

Finally, when we stopped at a red light, he looked over his shoulder and asked me if I was Chinese. After I answered him, he asked me where I was born. I told him. He turned his head, snorted as if he were a horse, and said: You are not Chinese, you are an American. There's no Chinese left in you. He repeated this when he learned that I didn't speak Chinese either. I must have stayed too long in the bar, because I feel as if I had pissed away some part of my identity without even knowing it.

It was clear that the cabby thought it was disgraceful that I hadn't learned to speak Chinese. For if I had, then it wouldn't have been so bad that I was an American. Maybe I would have had a shred of Chinese floating around somewhere inside me—a piece of pink confetti left over from the New Year's parade of swirling dragons.

As I paid him, stingy with my tip because I don't like cabbies or waiters who insult me, he didn't seem to notice how little I had given him. He just looked at me like I was some kind of dumb snake and he was the clever mongoose, and proudly announced: I'm Chinese. I guess this was supposed to drive the snake back into the basket. I was born there and I speak the language. You are only an American. That's all. Just an American.

I could still hear him rambling on after I slammed the door and began walking away. I didn't feel like telling him that my father speaks Chinese, lived there for many years, but didn't write it and wasn't born there. That his mother was English. Or that my mother was born there, that she had studied Mandarin and believed that those who were born in Shanghai were infinitely superior to those who weren't. Like talking to my parents, I knew this conversation couldn't go any further than it had.

My mother is a short, fat woman who cannot talk with Chinese waiters. She speaks a different dialect. They're from Canton, she tells me each time we go to a Chinese restaurant. I do not speak Cantonese. When the waiter comes over, she hands him a piece of paper on which she has written our order. She smiles as the waiter walks away. Let's hope they know how to read it, she whispers loudly to everyone at the table.

There is one question I can count on when I meet someone for the first or second time. Can you speak Chinese?

And always, their response is the same. Oh really, that's too bad, each of them replies when I tell them that my parents never taught me to speak or write Chinese.

Usually, a spasm of sympathy, resembling an imploding sneeze, passes through their facial muscles. But when they look down, somewhat despondent, as if they just received bad news, I'm always quick to change the subject. I don't want to go into the details of why I don't speak or write Chinese. I don't want another display of sympathy to fill the air between us.

To be exotic in America means that you possess uncommon looks, as well as a language and way of thinking that is utterly mysterious to others. In my case, I am semi-exotic. Something less than Ivory soap, but something more than fruit punch.

Hello, I am your basic, inscrutable fruit punch. You can't quite guess what went into it, but you're not afraid to try it out, are you?

My advice. don't try this line out on a woman you

meet at a bar or a party. At least not right away. She'll look at you like you're crazy.

Has it ever occurred to you that everyone in America is exotic to someone? Yes, but this kind of thinking can't be sustained for very long. Why not? Well, think of the consequences. How would you talk to anyone? What would you say?

A Pakistani cab driver told me that he was tired of being mistaken for an Arab. Why does everyone think I'm an Arab? he asked me. I'm not a Moslem, I'm a Hindu. I don't know anything about camels. I've never even been to the zoo in this stinking, fucking city of yours. Las Vegas is in the desert. I don't go to Las Vegas and try and make piles of quick funny money. Go see desert from air-conditioned limo. I pay good money for the gas that goes into this piece of crap. You think this is a cab. Well, it's not. It's shit a dog wouldn't smell.

If I were a mushroom, things would be different. I would look like something else, but I would be fatal to whoever failed to see the subtle differences. In my case, the reverse is true. I do not look like other mushrooms, but I seem on the surface at least to act like them. I drink coffee in the morning, for example, and I brush my teeth on a fairly regular basis.

One morning, this was when I was still married, my wife

116

turned to me, batted her eyelashes, and said that she had had a wonderful dream.

Yes, last night I dreamed that I was Chinese. I entered this big room and looked in a beautiful, gold-framed mirror above a white marble mantelpiece and saw that it was true, that I had become Chinese. This must be because I've been looking at you so much since we got married that I am starting to forget what I look like.

I wasn't sure what to say. What do you say to a blonde woman from Connecticut who tells you that she thinks she's becoming Chinese? What do you say to your wife when she tells you she has forgotten what she looks like?

It must have been something you ate last night.

Don't be silly. I think this is an important dream. I think it says something momentous about our relationship.

After a few seconds thinking about what she had just said, I must admit that I was stumped. Momentous, I said cautiously. By now I am standing in the bathroom, looking in the mirror, trying to wake up. In fifteen minutes I have to leave to see my shrink. I can't tell him about my dream in our session because I didn't have a chance to remember it.

Yes, momentous. Don't you think this dream is an indication of how close we've become? After all, I now think that I'm Chinese.

I'm squinting in the soap-streaked bathroom mirror, trying to focus, because I haven't put my contact lenses in. I know I don't see a blonde woman, but I'm not sure what I do see. Something resembling a potato with black moss growing wildly out of its top. I wonder what it means when a nearsighted, forty-year-old Chinese-American male of mixed parentage sees a hairy potato in the mirror. I mean potatoes

117

aren't Chinese, they're Irish. Didn't the English used to think that the potato was some kind of aphrodisiac, and that the reason the Irish had so many children was because they ate lots of potatoes? What do you learn from knowing this, I ask myself. It's easy. The English don't like sex and they don't like potatoes. How can you make such a large generalization?

Wait a minute, does my wife think she's English or Irish? I know she's part something and part something else, but what? Oh yes, of course. She's Scottish and English, not quite a descendant of the pious pioneers who boarded the *Mayflower,* but close enough. That's when I decide not to tell my wife what I am seeing as I look in the mirror. She'll think I'm making fun of her, and I'm not.

A few days later my wife brings up the dream again. She has a faraway look when she tells me that she's glad she had that dream.

I am beginning to get annoyed, though I am not sure why. You know it was just a dream, I tell her. I mean dreams are important, but what they seem to say and what they're saying may be two different things. Of course, the minute I say this I want to burst out laughing. Instead, I smirk to myself.

What's so funny?

Oh, I was thinking that I must be starting to sound like my shrink. I suppose when you begin sounding like your shrink, that doesn't mean you're making progress. It simply means that you have learned how to imitate someone's language without exactly knowing what it means. Suppose you name your dog Stupid. He might learn his name, but you can rest assured he's not going to wag his tail and drool if he knows what you're really calling him. Unless, he's a masochist of some kind.

Well, you can think what you want. But I know it's true.

What's true?

It's true that I dreamed that I was Chinese.

So.

Well, it's a known fact that you can't have a dream in which you die. You can almost die in a dream. You can come really close, fall out of an airplane or off a building, whatever. But you can't actually die. You never hit the earth. It's one of those things that can't happen in a dream, because if it did, you wouldn't wake up. You'd be dead. So if you dream that you're Chinese, it means that it can really happen to you. I mean it must be obvious to you by now that I have started becoming Chinese. Besides, why is it so hard for you to believe that I'm becoming Chinese? Dreams can come true, isn't that something your mother always says? Well, are you afraid she might be right? What are you afraid of anyway? Can you tell me that?

A friend once told me a story about a very rich man in the Midwest who built a house that resembled a pagoda, except that its interior dimensions were based on an oversized ranch house. Over the years, he and his wife accumulated lots of authentic Chinese knickknacks, all of which they carefully displayed. They ate with chopsticks off of Chinese dishes and collected rare books on Chinese art and antiquities. Although his butler, maid, and cook were from South America, they did not seem to think it was odd that this American couple acted as if they were Chinese. Maybe they thought all Americans were a little strange or maybe they just needed the job.

The cook even learned to cook fancy Chinese meals exactly the way the man and his wife liked them.

Anyway, he and his wife wore embroidered silk robes and black slippers around the house. On Sundays, they listened to Chinese opera or folk music, while following the intricate plots with the help of various books. Although they had never been to China, much less Hawaii, they seemed to know a lot about the country, its people and customs. Certainly more than any of their neighbors.

One day a Chinese family moved into a house down the street, a ranch house in fact. They were not quite as rich as the couple who lived in the pagoda, but they were, like everyone else who lived on the street, extremely successful. Well, it seemed the oddest thing at the time, but the rich man and his wife never welcomed their new neighbors. They did not even bother to say hello to them when they passed them on the street. When someone asked the Chinese man about this, he smiled and said it was because they were from different parts of China.

My mother talks about Shanghai the way Manhattanites talk about New York City. People from Shanghai, she is proud to announce, are innately superior to people from the rest of China. They are probably superior to the people from the outlying boroughs, the Staten Island and Bronx of Shanghai, but I do not say this to her, because I know she'll be quick to agree.

My mother's hierarchy is as plain and simple as the black cotton coats the members of the Chinese government wear to official functions. I don't tell her that either. She believes the Chinese are better than everyone else in the world, and that the people from Shanghai are better than the rest of the Chinese. She was, as she likes to say, born on the apex of the pyramid.

I am leaving something out. Although my mother is from Shanghai, my father is not. In fact, he was born in New York City (the Shanghai of the West, as my mother likes to call it). His father was Chinese, he was even from Shanghai, but his mother, poor and lowly accursed creature that she was, had the misfortune of being born in Liverpool. My mother, who respects the English, but has never been to Liverpool, seems to think of the city as some sort of dilapidated housing project by the ocean. A slum. She likes to point out that neither Shakespeare nor Benjamin Disraeli, much less anyone from the Royal Family, had been born in Liverpool. For her the equation is simple, Liverpool rhymes with cesspool and Shanghai means paradise.

Sometimes, I think of asking my mother where I fit into her hierarchy, given that one of my grandparents is English. But then, knowing my mother as well as I do, I stop myself. With my mother, the best road is the one I do not venture down, the one I carefully tiptoe around.

A teenager once spat in front of me because he thought I was Japanese. It was a hot, muggy Sunday in July, and we were the only people standing on a grungy subway platform in Brooklyn, waiting to catch a ride into Manhattan. When I found out why he spat at me, I told him I was Chinese and he apologized.

I'm Chinese too, he said sheepishly. That's why I spit at you. I thought you were Japanese. You can understand my mistake, can't you? I mean, you do realize that you don't look Chinese, don't you?

Two friends and I were walking down a street in Caracas when a young girl came up to us, curtsied and said hello. She spoke English perfectly, but in a manner that seemed to have come from old movies rather than from growing up in America. Enchanted, we asked her where she had learned to speak so well. The girl hesitated and then said proudly, Iran. I am from Iran.

No, a voice interrupted her. We are not from Iran, we are from Iraq. Iraq, he said it again. How many times do I have to tell you that we are from Iraq. It was the girl's father. He had stopped at a vendor when she came running up to us and began talking. He must have heard what she said because he was suddenly beside her, holding her hand, scared and turning red in the cool winter evening. After he realized that we weren't his enemy, he relaxed for a moment and told us that he had moved to Venezuela to work for an oil company, and quickly got embarrassed again. Everything he said or thought of saying seemed to make him nervous.

This incident happened when Iraq and Iran were at war with each other, and Americans were supposed to secretly cheer for the Iraqi army. Now that the American government is angry at both of them, I sometimes wonder what the girl's father has told her to say.

The third time my wife told me about the dream, I told her that she might have made a mistake. Maybe she wasn't turning Chinese, maybe she was turning Japanese or Korean. She said I wasn't very funny.

There should be a space between two people where it is understood that they won't see eye to eye, and dance cheek to cheek, and maybe they never will. I do not know what you call this space, but it better be there. Otherwise, each of you will wake up one bright morning, holding the end of a rope and pulling.

I didn't learn this until after my wife and I got divorced. I don't know if she still talks about the dream she had, though somehow I doubt it. She certainly did for a few weeks during the two years we were married. But, during the months we have been separated, I have had many dreams. I've almost been hit by a garbage truck and I've been chased through a convent by a giant squirrel. But I do not remember ever being a blonde woman in any of them. I do not even remember looking Chinese.

Maybe, as she once announced, this is just further proof of your limited imagination. And then again, as I answered her, maybe not.

Clothes Make the Man

Tonight started out like a bird circling regally above the city. A crisp blue sky was glowing behind Lower Manhattan's rust-colored towers, the narrow streets of Soho turning blue and gold in the autumn light, its lengthening shadows. Clocks, cabs, and couples young and old holding hands—everything and everyone seemed as if they were obeying the majestic pace of the gliding, soaring bird.

I walked over to the Red Star because Sheila said she would meet me there around nine. It wasn't too crowded when I got there. George was tending bar and talking to the regulars about baseball and football, the end of one season and the beginning of another, giving them whatever made them happy.

"Hi George, give me the usual."

"Vodka and soda, twist of lime coming up, sir," he replied.

That's what George always calls me, "sir." I have no idea why, though I now suspect that, like Sheila, George saw right through me.

As I stood, waiting, I nodded my greetings to the

familiar, weathered faces. A minute or two later, George slid my drink across the bar, picked up the money I placed there and left. The world was moving the way I wanted it to, smoothly and always forward, like a clock. Soon I was going to become the person I never thought possible.

I sat at one of the tables and watched the other regulars leaning onto the bar, hunched down on their stools like aging race car drivers waiting for the checkered flag to fall. Soon I would leave this club of lonely men behind.

Leo was just across from me, holding down his spot at the far end of the bar, still doing the crossword puzzle, and sucking down his umpteenth vodka and grapefruit juice.

"Got to get my daily dose of vitamin C," he tells me whenever we sit near each other. "Yep, these little greyhounds keep the messengers of old age away," he laughs, pointing to a glass which George always keeps full.

Leo's one of those people who always manages to look both disheveled and fit. He's in his late forties and has sandy blond hair which could pass as a yacht owner's toupee. He says it's his own hair but I don't believe him. I think it came from a cocker spaniel and that he had it grafted on by some quack healer.

Leo's one of the three or four people you can count on finding in the Red Star in the late afternoon. He always comes in wearing a suit and he always makes a ceremony of taking off his tie right before he sits on the last stool at the far end of the bar. No one knows if he has a job or not, or even what job it could be since he seems to spend most of his time in here, drinking and doing the crossword puzzle. But Leo always pays in cash, tips well, and never complains about being broke.

Wally was sitting next to Leo, talking to a woman I never saw before. Every chance he could he leaned over and whispered in her ear, and, as he did so, slid his hand across her back or rubbed her thigh. Happy hunting, Mr. Masseur, I thought to myself.

Like Leo, Wally is in his forties and has a thick crop of salt-and-pepper hair and a grim smile. He's neither fit nor fat, but somewhere in between. A good-looking man on the brink of going to seed, women seem to fall in love with him, if only for the length of two or three drinks. It's his friendly hands that scare them away.

All of us like to sit as far away from the front door as possible. We like being in the back, where we can see everyone else in the place. I wouldn't say we do this in memory of Wild Bill Hickock or anything, that's too sophisticated.

You know those miniature green shrubs that grow in terrariums, the artificial light on day and night? That's us. Little green shrubs clinging to wet rocks and soft, moist dirt. Or, if we've evolved beyond plants, then we're fish, our mouths opening and closing as we swing back and forth in the tide, hovering in the shadows near slimy rocks.

The Red Star and The Aerodrome may only be a few blocks apart, but, as someone I know once said of a synagogue near St. Peter's, it took almost two thousand years for the Pope to walk from one to the other. Unlike the Red Star, there are no regulars over forty in The Aerodrome, which is a couple of blocks south of Canal Street and the two topless bars I used to go to late at night, before going to the bars with no neon lights and no name above the door. Windowless places with loud music and beefy bouncers who frisk you for weapons. Bars where nearly everyone comes in a costume: Batman, Mr. Daredevil, Little Lucy, and the Merry Widow all go there.

Six months ago, just before turning thirty, I stopped going to these places and cut back on my drinking. I decided I had to change my ways, though I couldn't figure out exactly what this meant. It's not like I wanted to become a model citizen or anything. It's just that I wanted to get out of a rut that I felt I was digging deeper and deeper. I wanted to get out while I still could and move over a few dozen feet or so, start another.

The night I met Sheila at The Aerodrome I was getting another drink when I saw an acquaintance, Betsy, sitting at a table. We had met a party full of writers and artists and somehow, amidst the cheerless camaraderie, we started talking to each other. In the months since then we always said hello, as if to reassure ourselves that we once had a meaningful conversation.

Betsy and Sheila were disagreeing with each other about something when I walked over to their table. It wasn't private, but esthetic, so they didn't mind stopping where they were and inviting me to sit down. I went back to the bar, got my drink, and joined them.

Betsy was trying to finish her first novel. "I'm an only child and it's about four sisters," she told me at the party. When I sat down and asked her how she was doing, she brought me up to date. "One of the sisters has died since I last saw you, but the others are moving right along. Who knows? Maybe they'll all be there in the end. If the book ever gets published, I'm having a party for them and me."

Sheila told me she was talking to a new young dealer about showing her photographs. "Conceptually speaking, they're about the occult presence of radiation in the deepest corners of our lives, the ones where even the dust can't reach."

I didn't try to press Sheila for more information because it would've meant that I didn't really understand what she was talking about, something you didn't admit to in the downtown scene. I just sat there, trying to act both curious and interested. Or maybe inspired and understanding. I knew some combination was the right one. I hoped it was the one I could summon forth, the one I had handy.

They were, they announced simultaneously, planning their seasonal assault.

I didn't say what I was doing because I wasn't sure that I was doing anything. My answer to any inquiry about what I'm doing has always been pretty much the same: "Oh, the usual. A little of this and a little of that."

My friends and I don't want to admit it, but there are two problems we have to face. We may be artists or writers, but we still believe in upward mobility. Only some of us think that making it in this town is a sign of corruption, while not making it is an act of integrity and heroism. But the ones who keep saying that the geography of Lower Manhattan is made up of two poles, corruption's filthy lucre or heroism's impoverished purity, are really just jealous. They want to live someone else's life. They want to trade their honesty card in and they're pissed off that no one is making them an offer.

The other problem is a bigger one. Being an artist or writer means you may one day get your work reviewed in the newspaper. You may even be mentioned in the gossip columns, but the fact is, you're still a small fish in a very big sea. You might say that artists and writers live in a pond. Some of them get to jump into a nearby lake. A few, a very few, make it all the way to the ocean. But that's another geography lesson and I'm not sure that I believe it. I'm not sure what I believe in, except that maybe some people believe in me. That's what Sheila knew about me that first night. But their belief, its mirror, is what I've never been able to face.

Sometime later, Sheila and I started meeting at the The Aerodrome, Red Star, and other downtown bars. It was always just for a couple of drinks, and a long, slow descent that never quite touched bottom. We were flirting with the bottom, as well as each other. A quiet flirtation, almost as if two other people were saying these things, leaning towards each other without quite pressing their bodies together. Our flirtation filled the air between us with the perfume of what could be, but wasn't. At least not yet.

On the surface, our conversations were about books, movies, exhibitions, and gossip. Who did what when. What was said. Who did he become when he wasn't him. That kind of thing. Both of us knew that art and literature can be used to say lots of things, and it was those things that kept lingering, unsaid, that compelled me to call her once and sometimes twice a week.

What did I want to say or hear? If I close my eyes and think about it, I realize our flirtation, our talking around each other's lives, was a form of intimacy I pretended to find satisfying. There were two problems, however. It couldn't stay that way, and I didn't know that I was pretending to be something I wasn't. Eventually or maybe inevitably our flirtation started swirling around us, like a storm. And, like a storm, it became something larger than either of us. But in the beginning, in the first few weeks Sheila and I hung out, everything seemed fine. We were in a story that ended where it began, the kind of story I thought I felt comfortable putting back on the shelf

At the end of the night, Sheila would hail a cab and head back down to her place in the financial district. I would walk north to my apartment, sometimes stopping at another bar, sitting in a quiet corner, and drinking a beer. I wanted just enough alcohol to keep me high, maybe even raise me a little higher, but not enough to push me off whatever pinnacle I had reached. True, it was a pathetic pinnacle, but it was the only one I was sure I could manage.

No. Maybe it happened differently. A couple of days or hours ago, I would have told you that I kept feeling as if Sheila were pulling me toward her, that she was the North Pole and I was a piece of shiny metal. Tonight I don't know what's pulling me toward her, only that I'm being pulled.

One morning, a couple of months ago, I kept hearing children giggling, which made me think I was hallucinating since there was no one in the room with me and no children in the other apartments on this floor. Then, I heard one of them say: "Look, there's a naked guy over there."

I walked to the window and looked out. I live on the sixth floor so I'm hanging out the window when I realize that I was the naked guy the kid was talking about. There they were, a bunch of kids standing by the window in the parochial school across the street from my apartment, a couple of nuns too. All of them looking at the strange man with no clothes on.

Had I forgotten about the school? Or had I never thought about the fact that there was a school across the street? Was this the first time they saw me? Or had they seen me before, stumbling around my apartment, lost in a fog? I must have only thought about them when I heard them, when they were a nuisance. Otherwise, they were invisible. And I suppose I believed I was invisible as well.

When Sheila walked through the doors of the Red Star, she was wearing a dress so thin everyone could see the fullness of her breasts and long muscular legs. She was like a dancer floating inside a curtain, someone you would want to photograph from every angle so that when nobody was looking you could hold it, fondle it, maybe even lick the dust off. That's where I thought the evening was going.

We began drinking and looking at each other. She stretched out her long legs so they were on either side of me. We sat at a small square table, my knees pushing against the edge of her chair. She slid down, squeezed my legs between hers, and then sat back up again, and smiled.

"I've been thinking that we should try a little experiment tonight," Sheila began.

"An experiment?" I repeated, puzzled and intrigued. I could feel ants marching through my veins.

"Yes, an experiment. The kind that will change our lives forever. Are you interested?"

"Sure," I answered, thinking that Sheila always did talk like this. I looked at her and then at my drink. I wasn't sure what else to say, and Sheila knew it. She smiled, two rows of perfect teeth. The kind you see only on television or in the movies.

I felt as if I were floating on some strange river, drifting through a landscape I had never seen before. The air was full of the sound of birds. Or was it the other people in the bar, all of them paying attention to something else, things that did not concern us? I smiled, but it felt forced. This was not how I expected the evening to go. Did I know how it would go? Have I always been this foolish and arrogant?

The whole time Sheila didn't say anything. She just smiled and then picked up her drink, fiddled briefly with the straw, and drank.

132

We didn't go to Sheila's place or mine. We walked around for a while, arm in arm, like a happily married couple. Then we stopped and kissed in an alley. I remember my hands sliding down her back, and feeling the thin fabric clinging to her shoulder blades, her skin. Soft blonde down just above her lip.

Somewhere in New York, Hong Kong, or Berlin a movie was filmed on a dark street. A man and a woman are caressing each other in the shadows, which have been carefully accentuated by the floodlights the director has placed in key spots. The shadows have as much weight as the things they touch. Fragments of the couple's intimacy flash by on the screen. Weight of breasts against cloth, against skin. Bright beads of sweat rolling to the edge of a leaf or lip. Hands slipping beneath and between, opening and closing. Rustle of clothes. Tongues and teeth. Knees and legs. All through this encounter there is no music to distract the viewer, only the barely heard sounds of the couple's breathing.

The film dissolves.

When the film starts again, the couple is standing by the curb, under a streetlamp, and she is on her toes, whispering in his ear. "I know you want to come home with me." Her words are wet and round. "I want you too. I want you to climb into my bed wearing a nightgown and lingerie. I want you to have on lipstick, powder, and eyeliner. Once you do all of that, I'll be all yours."

The woman's painting a picture and the man's watching her fill in the colors, shapes, and forms. There are jagged lines and soft ones. There are promises and hints. A very large room at the end of a long hall, she tells him. An elevator that rises quietly to the ninth floor.

Before she can finish, a cab pulls up, and she turns and walks towards it, opens the door and gets in.

He's standing in the street, looking at her. She smiles and throws him a kiss. The cab screeches off.

I didn't stop in any bars because there was no one I wanted to see or talk to. I just walked home, climbed the stairs to my apartment, opened the door and walked into the dark kitchen.

Now I'm lying on the floor listening to the hum of the refrigerator. I'm holding a can of beer, as if it's a cold, wet stone, and I don't know whether I should put it down or throw it. I haven't bothered to take off my clothes because that would mean the day is over and it's not.

It's really simple. I've never made anyone happy. I've never even turned out the way anyone hoped I would. I'm neither a success nor a failure. I'm something without a name.

Yes, it's true. I'm going to change my membership. From now on, I'll be exactly what you want. I'll wear a pale pink slip and a double loop of milky white pearls. I'll wear anything you got in your closet or bureau. Why, Sheila honey, I'm ready to be your one and only little darling, the one whose picture you'll keep in your purse.

Family Album

I like to watch a woman undress, while my brother likes to wear women's dresses. We both seem to like tight dresses, though I suppose my tastes are not as refined as his. Or my tastes tend toward one kind of tightness and his toward another. It is not something we have discussed.

I know there are families where such things are discussed. I've seen them on afternoon talk shows. I once spent a month in Florida, near Daytona, teaching morning classes to fledgling writers, two of whom claimed to be in mid-career but were simply frozen in mid-flight. I'd come back from class and spend the rest of the daylight hours watching television, trying to see what family resembled my own. Some days they all did. Other days I wasn't sure.

I would keep thinking that the people who were telling their life stories were not even like anyone I knew. Does this mean I'm the one who is strange and weird? Or does it mean that they're the freaks, the maladjusted, the emotionally and mentally lame? Maybe we've lost our emotions, what's left of them, and the real reason we watch and listen to obese mothers, topless dancers, bossy boyfriends telling us their sadly ordinary tales is because we're desperate to get them back? We want to know that they can cry and laugh and mean it.

There are some things you think you will never mention to anyone, not even your closest friend, but one day you begin talking about them. One day you begin talking about them, knowing that it is not what you want to be doing, but you go on talking, go on as if there is nothing else to talk about, as if you were talking about someone else, someone you made up.

Made up, I think. It is not something I made up, it is someone he makes up, someone in make-up. He makes himself up as he puts on his make-up. It is not make-believe, it is someone he makes up, someone he sees looking back from the mirror, looking back from that place in which he is encased, frozen face covered in something other than ice.

Is the face he sees in the mirror the one he wants, the secret one inside him? Or is it the face of the one who judges him, the one who holds a whip over him and makes him beg for mercy? What about the face I see in the mirror? The one behind the one everyone sees, the one I keep locked inside myself, like an unwanted child in a closet.

I'm sitting on the floor in my apartment, looking at the photographs, knowing without wanting to know that the talking had already started, that the voices have already entered my thoughts, have already become part of what I will or will not say. Now they are inside me too, photographs of my brother hanging in chains, wearing a shiny black dress, kissing the red shoes of a blonde woman, long black whip dangling from her gloved hand.

In Florida, I spent my days watching television, looking for someone who resembled my brother. Someone who will tell me what he couldn't, cannot tell me. And all the stories I heard and lives I saw were neither his nor mine.

I had slipped the photographs out of the envelope, expecting to see something else. An image of myself standing on the steps of my high school, twenty-five years after I graduated without honors of any sort, not an image of my brother hanging naked from the ceiling. My friend, Bobby, had taken these photographs of me the day my father was buried. We had driven back to my high school, talking about the days when we were friends, when our parents, all of them now dead, knew each other and had hopes and dreams. We were glad that our childhood was gone, glad that we could return to it when we wanted, and leave when we had to.

It was only later, while driving back to my parents' house, that I realized that I had started telling myself that the story I was in would be different now that my father was dead, now that his voice, like my mother's, would no longer fill my nights and break open my days. The photographs of me standing in front of my school were proof that I had finally graduated, that I had finally moved out of their house. All I wanted were the photographs. It was as if they proved something, that I could walk around my high school without being afraid, that I could leave it without being ashamed.

I had opened the envelope shortly after leaving the store. It was late in the day. I was walking down a crowded street, and had carefully lifted the photographs out, like a new deck of cards, and had started fanning them open in my hands. I didn't know who I was looking at, I didn't know this dark-haired woman smiling at me like an old friend. Then I stopped, and I looked more carefully, and I realized it was my brother who was looking at me, and we were both seeing someone else. I began walking faster, the envelope and

137

photographs shoved into my pocket, clutching them so they would not get away.

You can watch them on television and you can hear their sobs and justifications, but you cannot speak of the deprivation of someone else as if it is something that happened to you, something you own. You cannot speak of the events that marked you or your brother, the things that made each of you up, the make-believe rooms the both of you entered in order to get away from the ones you were in. You cannot tell either his story or your own. This is what I thought at first. This is where I wanted to stop.

So you sit there looking at the photographs of your brother hanging in chains and wonder what you can say to him or anybody else about what you are looking at. You wonder who would listen to you if you began. You wonder why. You wonder what you would say, and why you would say it. You cannot speak for others, you tell yourself. You cannot take their place. So you try and speak about the distance between here and there, about the space that will never grow smaller. The one between you and the television and the one between you and your brother. You are watching something and someone and you do not know who they are or why.

Yes, my brother is the one hanging in chains and I am the one looking at him. He is floating in the air, like a dead man, and I am lying on the floor. A wood-paneled room of a house in the suburbs, a one-room apartment in lower Manhattan. I am the brother who left his parents' house while still in high school, my brother is the one who moved back there after college.

Two sons. Neither of them got away.

I remember speaking to my parents about my brother and that they laughed. I was, as they pointed out, a writer, an unpublished writer, so what did I know about the world. Writers told stories. I was telling them a story. My story was not about a brother who was hanging from a ceiling, I didn't know this about him then, but about a brother who seemed to be bothered by something, who seemed to have something on his mind. What did I know about other people's problems? they asked, when I had so many of my own.

Though my brother has never admitted it, he is angry with me because his father loved him and his mother hated him, and he was stranded between their orbits. He believed his father was a weak, whining man, while his mother was a strong, stubborn woman. These things I know are true, and I don't need my brother to tell me them.

I, on the other hand, had been loved by a mother whose fierceness and fantasies knew no bounds, and hated by a father whose anger and resentment never subsided. Does my brother know this? Or does he think I am making them up, that this is the make-up I live in and cannot wash away?

Or was it different than I remember it? A mother who told her son what he could and could not dream about, a father who said all his son's dreams were worthless wishes. Maybe this is true for my brother, too.

Or maybe my mother told my brother he could not dream at all, and my father said that dreams seldom if ever come true.

Or was it that my brother was loved and hated in other ways, by parents I would never know? Ways that are lodged in my imagination rather than my memory, because I left as soon as I could, leaving them all behind. I had gone with my mother's blessings or so I thought until the phone calls began, until I began listening to the endless tears and tales of how much had been sacrificed on my behalf.

Or is this all part of what I wear when I walk down the street, and enter rooms full of faces unlike my own? And not something my brother knows.

Once I wrote a story about a brother waiting for his older brother to return, an older brother he imagines having, and who left before he was born. His abrupt departure caused his parents to become what they had become, two listless shadows staring into themselves, two mouths speaking about what life was like before he was born. In my story, the younger brother is sitting alone on the porch, watching cars pass. It is late evening, near fall. The light has started to change. He hears his parents shuffling around the kitchen, the murmur of their voices. He imagines that this will all change once his brother returns home, once he comes and rescues them from themselves.

After finishing the story, I put it away and didn't read it again for many months. I told myself I had written a story, and I had wanted to write something else, something that would hold something of myself inside of it, something I had not been able to inject into what I had written. A secret perhaps, something I could never tell anyone because I was embarrassed or ashamed. Was this when I first learned (but I did not listen to this voice then) that I could not escape into words, that I could not become a thing frozen in a white page of snow, that I would always be the one outside the story, the one writing or reading it?

Was it that I wanted to tell a story that held a secret inside of it? something that I was holding inside myself, something that I had not been able to speak about, that I had learned to believe it was wrong to speak about?

Was it that I wanted to put the face I held inside myself inside the story, lock it in that closet forever?

Or was it that I believed something else should be written? that the time for telling stories was over? that all the stories had been told?

Did I believe what I had been told about telling and because of that could not begin to tell?

Or had I for many years tried to escape into words and failed? Was I unable to become an object held up to the light? Couldn't not become a thing I saw from a great distance? A page of snow glistening beneath lamplight?

Or now, seeing the form of my brother's escape, I am wondering what I could say to him? Can you say anything and everything to anyone? Or must you make it up?

One morning, I fished the story out of my desk and began reading it. What I thought was about someone else, someone I made up, was about me and my brother, the one hanging in chains, the one in the photographs I had been holding, the one who never answered any questions. Who are these people inside me? — the man who likes to watch a woman undress, a man who likes to wear women's dresses, a woman who likes to strike men or tie them up, a mother who insists, a father who screams as he pushes you to the floor. Why are all of us down on our knees praying? hoping that our wishes come true, and not realizing that they have.

In the story I had written, the older brother does not return. In the story I have not written, the one which has written me, I am the older brother who does not lower his brother to the floor. Rather, in this story which is still writing itself down, the brother hanging from the ceiling writes the same story over and over. He has not found a way out of

141

his story. He has not found a way to release himself from its words. He has not found a way to make the ending change. I am this person's brother. The one who tells the stories, but who cannot make the ending change.

My brother stays inside the story in which he makes himself up in a room of make-believe. He is listening to himself tell a story and he is playing all the parts. It is a story no one else, neither me, the one looking at him, nor the blonde woman behind him, the one looking at the camera, has ever really heard. It is a story told to him over and over again until finally he believes that there is no other story but the one he is in, and begins telling it to himself and no one else. What I and the woman in the photograph hear are the bubbles of a deep sea diver reaching the ocean's surface, the silence of the one below.

One brother hanging inside the words of others, and one brother trying to escape into words he thinks are his own. This is our story, I thought. This is one that my brother has never heard.

Did my brother endure my father's humiliation? Or does he feel like he should repent because he didn't? Was my mother the one who used the belt on him? Had he, like me, been beaten many times? Or had he been beaten by words rather than by a belt, broom, or brush? How many times is too many? I think. When is enough more than enough? How far is too far?

Once, while writing a letter to my father detailing each of the times I remembered clearly, I thought I should stop because I never spent a night in the hospital. Was I, as my father insisted right up to the morning he died, stubborn and spoiled? Was I, as my father repeated on his death bed, a worthless nothing? There are some questions you cannot answer and others you should never hear, but you do.

My brother has never said if he read the letter I mailed to my father, the letter my father read to my then wife, a painter who believed it was possible for a blonde Yankee from Connecticut to become the child of Chinese immigrants, like her husband. My brother has never mentioned that my wife stayed with them during Christmas, and they had all spoken of the older brother's repeated desertions. My brother has never talked about my blonde, blue-eyed wife, a former high school cheerleader and cum laude graduate from a fashionable all girls' college, a painter who doesn't wear make-up and believes she has started to look and think Chinese.

My brother has never told me that our father gave our dead mother's jewelry to my wife. As he said to me later, I didn't deserve to have these things because I was stupid and stubborn and had left my wife, who was a far better person than I could ever be.

Later, on the phone, my wife would tell me that she had been surprised by the calm, matter-of-fact tone of my letter, that my father had said to her after she had read the letter that I was very spoiled when I was young, and that I was still spoiled or I wouldn't have left her. She would ask me why I couldn't see what had happened to me from my father's point of view. She would ask me when we could see each other again? She would ask me why I had run away from her? Why I wasn't happy? What had she done? She would say that I didn't need to be afraid of her and that she only had my best interests at heart.

I didn't tell her that we could have told our stories on television. I lay on the bed and listened. I looked at the ceiling and wondered if I would ask her why she had not mentioned the things my father gave to her, the things my mother once wore, the things she had managed to carry with her when she left China, when she left her parents and a city turning to smoke and ash. And when she didn't, I knew that it didn't matter if she were better than me or not, because I had nothing else to say to her, that the question I had never asked and what she never said formed a wall between us, and that jewelry my father gave her belonged to her because she wanted to badly to keep what was never hers.

Do you or anyone else have to be there to know what actually happened? Is this what must happen for you to know what actually occurred in this room or that? The stories that never get told, the ones that each of us has kept. Are these what must secretly be repeated in order for us to pass safely through each day?

I am looking at the photographs, but I am not in the room in which they were taken, basement of a suburban ranch home, formica paneling, and a bleached blonde in a red leather skirt, white satin blouse, and purple sunglasses, holding a whip and smiling. I am looking at the photographs of someone who could be a relative of my wife, a poor sister or country cousin.

I am thinking of the sunglasses my wife wore at the beach, when we were in the Bahamas, of the wooden walls of her parents' house, of the lies they tell about their marriage. I am looking at the photographs and thinking that though the blonde in purple sunglasses, the blonde smiling into the camera, looks like a poor relative of my wife's, that she is not, and that neither her story nor my wife's are mine to tell.

I see the bleached blonde's thin-lipped smile, but not her eyes. I can hold the photographs and try and rock myself to sleep, but I can't hear what my brother and the blonde are saying to each other when the camera is pointed the other way or is sitting on a shelf. There are some words you have no way of hearing, and others you have no way of either shutting in or out.

This story, I tell myself, is the one I must tell, the one whose flame is burning through the film, turning it into ash in my hands. It is the story of two brothers. One brother knew he had been hit many times, the other brother never mentioned whether he was hit or not. One brother wants to talk but doesn't know how, the other brother whispers to himself. The one who is trying to learn to talk likes to watch a woman undress, while the one who knows only how to whisper to himself likes to wear women's dresses. Each is owned by a pain he cannot share, however many other people are in the room watching. One moves from house to house, while the other sneaks into the same basement again and again. Neither of them speak of these things when they speak.

I spend my afternoons watching television, hoping to catch a glimpse of someone I know, someone who resembles me down to the last muffled whisper, the last theatrical tear.

Things You Said to Me When We Were Lost

If I'm anything, I'm an exhibitionist. I like people to watch what I'm doing, even when, or the more likely truth, most especially when I don't know they're actually watching. Once my boyfriend and I made love in a gully, and on the rim around us there were lots of people, mostly from the picnic we had been dragged to, my boyfriend and me. We didn't want to go to it, but in the end we were glad we did.

There's some things you do, and you don't know why until later. I do them, then I find out why. Or I figure out why before I do them. It seldom happens that one does and knows why at the same time.

You see we knew they were up there, sunbathing, sitting around, playing cards, or talking or reading. A bunch of middle-aged idlers. Some of them probably noticed what we were doing down there. Anyway, no one ever said a word to me or to my parents. It was like it never happened. They were scared to say it happened, because they knew neither my boyfriend or I cared what they saw or thought. Hell, if I had cared just a little bit about what they saw or thought they saw, they would have felt it was their business to say something hot and mean to me. They would have started off smiling, but ended up calling me all sorts of names. Or they would have stood around and whispered behind my back, like a basket full of snakes. But I got sick of listening to other people's slop swilling around when they spoke, a bunch of pinched, bloodless faces looking down at a child and saying all that well-meaning stuff like they thought I was stupid enough to believe it. Who would want any child to be that stupid?

There's lots of things I've never done before, but that doesn't mean I won't do them. It's the things that I know I won't do that tell me something about who I am. I remember reading something a porno actress said. She didn't do animals. You know why. Because she could never be absolutely sure if the sex was between two consenting adults when one of them was a dog.

I'm the person standing behind the door you're afraid to open. I don't know how I know this, but I do. Haven't you ever been that way? Haven't you ever known you were right when there was no way you could know? I haven't been right that many times in my life. Enough to be here, if here is where I think it is. But about this, I'm right. I know I am.

Somebody says to me, how do you like them apples? I say,

like these. Solid and soft. That usually gets a whimper out of them.

At one point or another in their lives, all men want to dress up in women's clothes. Some are just better about admitting this little secret to themselves. Then there's the others, you know, the ones curled up inside themselves, shrunken heads mounted on poles, their lips sewn shut. And how do I know about them? I'm a woman, that's how I know about them. I see them everywhere. And they're usually pointing at someone else.

I guess it's one thing to sleep with a dog, and another thing to sleep with a guy dressed up like a dog. The question I had to answer was simple. Which of these two things was I willing to do? That's when the little light went on, and I knew I was an exhibitionist.

A friend of mine makes money being a topless dancer. She likes getting paid and she thinks she's in control. I don't know about that, being in control I mean. Being in control means you're afraid to lose control. Me personally, I like leaving my body behind, as if it's a soft coat I took off and dropped on the floor. I get that feeling, I know I'm having fun.

I remember once being followed around by this guy in a brown suit. It probably had something to do with my boyfriend at the time. He was flirting with the bad end of bad trouble. And I just knew the guy must have been some kind of mucky-muck, one of those slaves to duty. You know why. His face looked like it had just been scrubbed with bleach. So all day I did things to let him know that I knew he was watching me. The kind of things that make a guy shift in his seat, break out in hives. You see, even reptiles with badges have a heart stuck in their pouch somewhere. But I didn't need to see his badge to know he was a reptile, because I had seen his teeth. A guy with a bleached face and teeth like that had to be working for the government. Who else would hire him?

I know a woman who stops and picks up every shoe she sees lying in the street. It can't be a pair of shoes. Just a single shoe. If she's driving on the highway and sees one, she pulls over, goes back and gets it. She keeps a diary of the ones she couldn't stop and get, and most times she returns to see if it is still there. She has a whole room in her house full of shoes, each one tagged as to where it was found. Sometimes she takes a snapshot of it before she picks it up. Doesn't know why she's doing it, but she's been doing it for years.

Did you read about that singer? He used to be in one of those folk groups. I can't remember which one. Then he went solo and had a couple of hits, nothing big. I still remember his voice, it was a blend of honey and broken glass. One day the dj's stopped playing his songs. I wondered why I didn't get to hear them anymore or why he wasn't writing and singing new songs, but no one seemed to know what happened to him. Well, the other day I read that this guy now runs a funeral service. He does burials at sea. Sails a boat full of boxes of ashes toward the sunset. Says he still sings, but the only ones listening now are them boxes.

I'm extremely flexible, cupped, and scant.

A guy with his tongue hanging out doesn't impress me much. Around here, a thirsty dog is a common sight.

I say if you can't tell someone something they want to know, then tell them something they don't know they want to know. You know why rumors start. It's because someone didn't tell someone else what they wanted to know.

They say dogs are loyal, but men are born cheats. You're supposed to be one of the lucky ones if you get a man and he's as loyal as a dog. He might be a dog, but he's the kind of dog you want following you around. Maybe, maybe not. I've seen lots of men walking around with their tails between their legs. They like to sleep on the porch all day, and they sure come running when it's time to eat. I don't like dogs very much. I think even less of their masters. My motto: A man who owns a dog is someone to be distrusted.

I come from that part of the world where men are fat and lazy lizards. Half the day they sit around, their tongues flicking bugs out of the air, like dirty neckties flapping in a hot wind. They got those eyes that blink once every two minutes, like a traffic signal on an empty street. The rest of the time they're staring at whatever is in front of them, wondering if the brains they were born with are ever going to come home. You know that football or baseball their little eyes lock in on, like radar? That's their brains leaving as fast as they can. Only a truly stupid man would cheer the guy running off with his brains or the guy clubbing it with a bat. Maybe they figure their brains are safe in there, all sewn up in leather.

I have to say this. It's easier to train a dog than a man. You get a dog when it's a puppy, and it's pretty easy to get it to listen. But anytime you think about getting into a recliner with a man, you have to remind yourself that he's already been housebroken in a house you wouldn't step foot in, much less get a glass of water from.

Most men think most women spend too much time shopping for clothes, getting dressed, and putting on their make-up. But they're worried the whole time, because if we don't make a good impression on everyone, they figure it will reflect bad on them. It's not that they're confused. It's that men are a kind of mirror, but they don't know which way it's facing. If you're a woman and you don't know which way you're facing, you better get your head and a lot else examined.

We all start out as exhibitionists. And, if we live long enough, we end up doing things we would never believe ourselves capable of doing. That's why I'm an exhibitionist. I like prolonging my infancy while getting a jump on my senility. I like doing two things at once, it saves time, not to mention wear and tear.

Inside each of us is an animal we might not want in our house. What you have to know is what kind of animal do you have roaming around inside you. What's the creature's name? What's it like to eat? Things like that. You don't know your animal, you don't know anything.

I got an animal inside me, but I'm not going to tell you its name. I do that, and you got a leash on me that will pull me anywhere you want to go.

It's not that I want to dance. It's that there's a dance we got to do. Sure you want to do something about it. But whatever you want to do isn't enough. The dance, that's what's calling us. Not me, not you.

One of my girlfriends wanted a baby, while her husband wanted a shiny new car. You think a baby buggy in the driveway is the answer. Or a mitten left in the rain. I was called away from that life by this one, and I came running.

One of my boyfriends told me I was certifiable. I told him a diploma is a diploma, it doesn't matter where it comes from.

The Language of Love

There are two cars, four adults, and two children. Or, to be more accurate. There are three women, one man, one boy, and one girl. The three women know each other, the man knows one of the women, and the boy and the girl have crushes on each other. The problem: how to divide this group up between two cars in a way that will make the long drive home pleasant. Or, if not pleasant, at least bearable to everyone.

I'm not particularly good when it comes to mixing math with people so I don't offer a solution to the rest of the group, because I figure one of them will sort it out. We're about to start driving back to Caracas from a small island in the Caribbean, where we've been camping out for five days. It's late in the afternoon, and the sun has started descending lazily towards the horizon, the shimmering turquoise blue ocean we're about to leave behind. We're headed towards the interior, towards the heavily patched and decaying two-lane highway that winds its way up the mountains to the new four-lane tunnel that connects the airport and coast to Caracas, which is in the valley on the other side of the mountains; a city full of tall office buildings, highrise apartment complexes, and exhaust fumes.

On clear days and evenings you can sit out on the patio, seven or eight stories above the constant din of automobiles and motorcycles, sip a martini, and look at the clusters of cardboard, crates, mud and tin shacks nestled a few miles away in the mountains. They're small enough that you might think they're just brown and orange rectangles in a green field. Or, if you are one of the lucky highrise residents who face another direction, you get to sit back and watch a sinuous, thick mass of clouds snaking through the sky just above one lush green mountain. And during the rainy season, on the days that are gray and heavy with moisture, a massive cloud bank usually sinks low enough to envelop the entire summit, as well as the ten-story hotel up there, that, for reasons too numerous to count, will never be completed; a needle-like bright red tower with shiny balconies for all the guests to sit on, as they enjoy their drinks and look down at Caracas, its crystal-like towers and soupy clouds of pollution. This is the only mountain near Caracas that isn't covered with rows and rows of shacks, and it is the view towards which most of us are headed.

The four adults: Carmelita, Carmen, Robin, and myself. The children are Juan, who is Carmelita's brown-haired son, and Clarissa, who is Robin's blonde daughter. I know Robin; and it's because of her I have met Carmelita, Carmen, and Juan, as well as gone on this camping trip. The result: Carmelita, Juan, Clarissa, and I are in one car, while Robin and Carmen are in the other. I'm pretty sure it was Robin who arrived at this equation, but I'm not one to argue because I know I'm the extra wheel.

Earlier this morning, on the launch taking us from the island to the hot, dusty lot, where, a few days earlier, we managed to park our cars in the shade under some palm trees, Robin told me she needed a break from Clarissa, that they hadn't been apart in five days.

"I need a rest," Robin sighed. "Sometimes, I need a rest. I haven't had a rest since my husband left me."

Robin is given to hyperbole, which may have been why I was initially attracted to her. She always knows how to dramatize her situation, make the most of a daughter's missing pink sock. I used to think that this was all I could understand; a person haunted by extremes, or, as Robin put it, the ghosts that chase you through your life.

Robin's nights and days were filled with ghosts. She was a mirror I could see myself in, a mirror which showed me that I hadn't quite fallen through the floor. Maybe on it, but not through it. There have been times in my life when the only women I was attracted to were those who, despite being in some kind of peril, always managed to get dressed up. I thought that dressing up was proof of their ability to resist chaos, that they managed to keep the chaos within.

I still don't believe I thought I was some kind of knight in shining armor. Far from it. You see, I believed that the only situation that was truly hopeless was my own. Maybe it's why I've never owned a sports jacket and I haven't worn a pair of shoes in years. I had given up trying to resist chaos. I welcomed chaos, particularly when it wasn't my own.

After figuring what was what and tossing our stuff into the right trunk, I hopped in Carmelita's car and told Clarissa to get in the back. She smiled, for she was all too happy to spend a few hours with Juan without her mother around.

It's hard to make rules for a child when you're not the

parent. I'm not a parent, and, when I was a kid, I never could follow rules much. It may have been why I bought Clarissa candy and stuffed animals and said okay too much of the time. Or it may have been a way to buy myself some of the things I wished I had been given when I was a kid. It doesn't take much to figure out why some people have children; they want a second chance. Every now and then in my life I've wanted a second chance, but I've never wanted to be a father. Being near someone else's kid is enough for me. It is usually the concerned parent I find troubling, not the screaming kid. Like I said, I can understand extreme behavior. It's when someone acts reasonable or, a favorite word these days, rational, that's when I begin wondering exactly what form of measure is being used.

I look over my shoulder, stare at the wriggling heaps in the back. Clarissa and Juan are wrestling, babbling away, and grinning like idiots. They are chattering in Spanish, something Clarissa refuses to do when she is around her mother. It makes me happy to hear her singing away and teasing Juan in his language, though I don't know why at the time.

Carmelita and I are slouched down in the front seats. She doesn't speak much English and I don't speak much Spanish. I can order chicken with rice, a cup of coffee, and a bottle of beer. When necessary, I can ask "Where's the bathroom?" Beyond that, I'm pretty lost. I'm not sure what Carmelita could order.

Every now and then one of us looks in the back to make sure the children haven't started playing "doctor" yet. That's the limit Carmelita and I seem to have set. Wrestling and loud singing are okay, but no nudity and muffled whispers.

I guess Carmelita and I have the same approach. Let the kids wear themselves out, but don't let them take their clothes off. Eventually, exhausted from their excitement, they will fall asleep, and the music coming from the tape deck will be the only sound inside this bright metal bubble zooming deeper into the night, the only sound, other than our hearts, we want throbbing beneath our skin. The music is like an extra heart, because it absorbs all the pain and then caresses it into comforting words one doesn't need to know in order to understand.

Carmelita has a brand new, bright red, fast American car. The tape deck is on loud, and a woman is begging her man to come back. I might not know Spanish well, and Carmelita might not know much English, but we both understand the music she slips into the tape deck. Most songs are like children, they make a sound you understand.

A soft sultry voice and a small fast car. I've always liked going fast, and I've always liked women who drive cars fast and smooth, as if they are preparing to be the one revving the engine outside a bank in Warren or Mentor, Ohio, one chilly November morning, a cold gray sky, and a quiet room full of unsuspecting tellers and clerks.

Carmelita is part Spanish and part Chinese. She and her family moved from the Phillipines to Venezuela when she was a small child. Her father had gotten a transfer from Manila, where he managed some kind of shipping company. He didn't want to stay in the Phillipines; he wanted to go to America. Caracas was as close as he got. He's muerte, dead, she tells me, and her mother, who is Chinese and Catholic, likes to stay up late and watch old reruns of popular American TV shows, particularly *The Flying Nun.*

While we were camping, Robin told me that Carmelita's mother sipped wine like a lady from another century. It was, she said, fantastic to be with her, because she was someone who remembered a way of living that no longer existed. Robin seemed to think that I would like meeting her, because she was sure her life resembled my mother's. I didn't tell Robin that resemblance isn't always the best place to begin, and that I was more interested in what shows Carmelita's mother watched, and what else besides wine and television she used to escape the empty bed, a life of looking back.

I didn't even know she watched television all night long until Carmelita told you, Robin whispered, while we lay in our tent, listening to the wind and the ocean. I thought that you two would sit around and drink red wine from Chile and she would tell you about what it was like to be a Chinese girl growing up in the Phillipines. I could tell Robin thought it was strange that I was more interested in what television programs an old woman watches late at night than in hearing about her childhood, but I wasn't sure I could begin to explain why I wanted to know such things.

Juan is seven, Carmelita is maybe twenty-five, but she looks like she's still in high school. She has a soft round face and big liquid brown eyes, the kind you see in yearbooks. I am the scruffy American guy who is visiting Robin, an unemployed, recently divorced American woman, who lives across the hall from her friend, Carmen, in a highrise in a fairly respectable part of Caracas.

This might sound like it has the makings of a TV show, but no company would sponsor it. It's not funny enough and it's a little too real. Who wants to hear a young, attractive Venezuelan woman compare dictatorship to democracy? and happily conclude that the former has far more virtues than the latter. Or listen to a woman talk about a relationship that should have ended before it began? Who wants to listen to sentences that end in long, meaningful sighs? We don't want our lives to sound like a soap opera, but they do. And like the most popular ones, ours go on and on. But unlike the stars of those shows, we don't get paid to betray or be betrayed again and again. We become villains, but those who hate us don't feel like they're biting into a big, sweet, delicious apple when they do so.

What am I doing in a red car speeding down a decrepit highway in Venezuela with a woman who hates to be caught behind any slow moving vehicle? What am I doing with a woman who pushes the pedal to the floor so she can pass the buses crammed with sad-eyed men and women, the trucks full of oil, pigs, chickens, lumber, or fruit? What am I doing with a woman who thinks of all these familiar sights as irritating billboards to the life she is trying to leave behind?

Twenty years ago, around the time Carmelita was five, these rusted old cars and dented trucks were brand new shiny items parked on quiet streets in Brooklyn or the suburbs of Des Moines. Twenty years ago I thought my life would turn out different. But now, sitting in a car that passes everything else on the road, I hear myself wishing she would go faster and not stop in Caracas.

I'm dreaming, though I didn't know that then, because I think I'm someone in a car with a woman he can't say much to, on his way back to a city whose streets and neighborhoods he's just starting to learn, a city which has quickly lost its charm and become, like every big American city, a noisy gathering of unpredictable forces. Like the people sitting in the buses and trucks, I'm someone stuck in the dull and dusty hallways of my own history. In reality, this means I'm someone who left his wife and got involved with a woman whose husband had left her stranded in Caracas.

I met Robin at a party in New York eight months

after I left my wife. When my friends tell me that I am still on the rebound, and that I ought to be careful, I tell them that I've been on the rebound all my life. They see a friend of theirs spinning out of control, while I see a basketball bouncing in front of oncoming traffic. What they really want to tell me is that my new situation isn't going to work out, but they don't. What I don't tell them is that I know this one's not going to work out, and that it doesn't matter much. The last one didn't work out either. None of them have.

Robin was in New York trying to figure out how she could stay in Caracas.

"It's cheaper there," she told me.

"And it isn't like America," she said a few minutes later. "The Venezuelans are a friendlier and warmer people. They aren't greedy or cold like Americans, especially New Yorkers. My husband and I went down there years ago. I want to stay on, work with the people down there. I lived in the jungle with them. It wasn't easy, but I stayed with them and eventually learned to speak their language."

The people, I wondered to myself. Who are the people anyway? Do they have to live in the jungle to be people? What about us? Were we some kind of animal just because we lived in big dirty cities and ate meat with knives and forks? It's true, I hadn't eaten monkey or tapir, but then neither had Robin. Besides you don't need to go to jungle to eat such things. You just have to know what restaurant serves them.

But all this I kept to myself when we started talking. Maybe because she didn't have to tell me that her husband had left her. Her pale, watery blue eyes told me something had happened to her, that she was ready for something else to happen, and, if I were ready, we could be the something we wanted to have happen. We could be the story we wanted to be, that's what we thought to ourselves that night, and why we decided to see each other again. The problem was we were neither speaking the same language nor telling the same story.

In retrospect, it was easier to leave my wife than it was to get married. I got up one morning and said to myself today is the day. I certainly didn't say that when we talked about getting married. Sleepy-eyed, she rolled over and asked me where I was going. I told her I was going to see my shrink, something I did four mornings a week, and had been doing for five years. My wife and I had been married a little more than two years, but she said she could never remember what I was doing, that I was always busy doing something, and that it was too much for her to try and remember, particularly since she had so much else on her mind, and she chuckled and pretended to go back to sleep. I got dressed in the dark and left for my appointment.

A few months earlier I had woken up and we had gone through the same routine. It had become a skit, something I was supposed to laugh at when she teased me. I made the mistake of trying to tell her that I had gotten tired of laughing at her jokes, as well as accepting that she had forgotten why I got up early four mornings a week, dressed in the dark, and rushed down the stairs to the subway. I didn't tell her that if she didn't know where I was going and couldn't remember this detail after two years, then she had no idea whom she had married and it was time for me to go. I didn't tell her because I thought it was evident that she treated me like some guy who she had picked up in a bar and whom she would never see again when he left in the morning.

163

The way I looked at it, I was going to a shrink because it was my last chance to connect the wires in my head. Otherwise, I was going to walk into a fire one day. What kind of fire I didn't know, I just knew it was out there, and if I didn't get some kind of map in my head, I was going be swallowed up by something before I could get out.

The last time I had come close, it was too close. I wasn't drunk either. Every other time I could blame it on drink or drugs: the months in the hospital after I rammed a car into a tree; the heroin addict I met in a topless bar; the cab driver who chased me with a tire iron because I told him he should have stayed home that day and fucked his wife, rather than trying to fuck with me.

I woke up one morning and gave up alcohol and drugs. I figured it was time to go straight, that I had reached bottom and needed to come up for air, see daylight. It was right after my girlfriend, Sally, took her dog and the silverware and moved to Barcelona. This was before I was married. Back then, my friends didn't say that I got married because I was on the rebound and maybe they're feeling guilty now. Who knows? I've never asked them what they thought then. It's too far away and I'm not the same person I was then.

I went five long years without drinking or taking drugs. One night, while driving up a hill, in a hurry to get home, I decided to pass between the two motorcycles up ahead, but I ended up ramming into a moving van stopped at an intersection. The driver thought I was from Mars when I told him what happened, and I thought maybe he was right. I figured it was time to get the internal wiring checked out, see if I could get back to Earth. But, in order to do so, I needed to find out about the person who couldn't tell the difference between two motorcycles going sixty and a truck stopped at a traffic signal. Two days later I started seeing a shrink.

Maybe that's why I like women who drive fast. Or maybe it's just that I like to go fast, but I don't want to be the one driving anymore. I have a friend in Texas who has a black Porsche and whenever I visit him, I say, how fast can you make this little machine go? Show me your stuff, Buster. And we both laugh as we zoom down the highway. Yeah, I'm thinking to myself. Show me we can go through the wall and come out on the other side. Show me how this thing can part the Red Sea.

I went to see my shrink that morning, as if nothing was wrong. Two nights later I left my wife and moved into my office down the street, a little storefront where I made clay models of whatever the client wanted: a man flexing his muscles or a dog sitting on his haunches, waiting to be fed. That morning and the next I didn't say anything about my plans to move out to the kind-faced man who was helping me patch myself together. I took my silence to mean that I was going to be seeing him far longer than I expected, which I didn't mind, because at least he didn't ask me what I was doing in his waiting room four mornings a week.

When I told my wife it was over and that I was moving out, she looked at me as if I were a stranger who had taken over her husband's body, which was probably the closest she ever came to recognizing me. There were no tears, not in the beginning. Just phone calls and short, handwritten notes. Recently, her lawyer sent me a letter so I figure we have entered the phase where surrogates will do all our communicating. This is not a surprise, but a relief. There was no form of communication with which we were comfortable when we were married. Two people who could have passed for our twins did all the talking, while she was in her studio and I was in my office. They were the ones who seemed to get along so well, not us.

Carmelita has been driving nonstop for three or four hours when she sees a gas station and decides to pull in. The kids are asleep in the back, and the car with Robin and Carmen is nowhere to be seen.

The gas station is a stained cement oasis illuminated by a blue sign and a bright overhead spotlight; three aging, dust-coated pumps looking like shrunken tin copies of Easter Island monoliths greet us as we pull into the lot. Behind us, two long caterpillars of headlights and taillights wriggle their way up and down the mountain, through a thin mist or smog.

I get out and quickly walk into the bathroom, only to discover the light doesn't work. I try flushing the toilet, but that doesn't work either. I figure I'm lucky, because if it had started overflowing, I'm going have to use the sink and be out of there before anyone finds out. Then I figure the sink is going to have to do anyway, that it has to be cleaner than the toilet, which stinks and which I can't see. A dark, wet hole in a humid closet is not my idea of creature comfort. Some people like Robin can live in the jungle, but I'm not one of them.

The sink is by the door, and there's a crack of light coming from the gas station's blinking blue sign outside. It's not much, but it's enough to show me the sink is relatively clean. The room is hot and smelly and I'm sure that I'm going to get sick if I stay in there much longer.

I'm like some crazy gymnast, trying to hold myself

above the grimy sink, trying to take a quick but necessary crap. I know it's comical, a man with his pants down, balancing himself above a sink and shitting in it. I tell myself that necessity may be the mother of invention, but it's also the uncle of hilarity. Besides, I'm glad I'm not the next guy, because he faces an even stiffer challenge.

I get out of there quick, see Carmelita sitting low in the car, waiting. Tapping the steering wheel in time to the music. Who's singing? I wonder. What sweet, slow lament is filling the air she inhabits? I know Juan and Clarissa are still asleep in the back, entwined around each other like thick pieces of rope, because I don't see their heads bobbing in the window.

Trucks hauling their cargo, an occasional bus belching blue smoke, everything is thundering by, causing the ground to shimmer slightly. An acrid cloud of smoke and dirt hangs in the night air, like the last, indestructible remains of something that has been cremated.

I must have been thinking about it all along, but I didn't want to know what I was thinking. I wasn't quite ready to listen.

The third time I came to Caracas and stayed with Robin and Clarissa, she wanted her daughter to speak to me in Spanish. It was show-and-tell time, something parents seem to need to do with their children. In the kitchen, while she and I were getting dinner ready, she said that she wanted to see if Clarissa accepted me or not. "It's a little test. I just need to know where you stand in Clarissa's eyes."

After putting the dirty dishes in the sink and closing the patio door, Robin and I sat in chairs, like a queen and her prince. Clarissa stood in front of us, a bright little puppet. She smiled weirdly at first and then began speaking gibberish. I started laughing, I didn't know what else to do, while Robin admonished her daughter, who was by then rolling on the floor, giggling and chattering, a nervous pile.

Later that night we argued. I told Robin that I didn't think she should've made Clarissa perform, and she thought that meant that I was telling her that she was a bad mother, that she was a failure. Somehow I had become the villain, the one who didn't understand what she had been through. I didn't argue because I agreed with her. One doesn't understand what someone else has been through, but that's not the point.

"But a marriage which doesn't work out isn't a failure," I told her.

"It is if you were once in love," she said grimly.

There are certain things you should never let become food for competition. One of them is the past. The past is always growing too fast for anyone to be able to eat it all. I didn't know then why everything that happened that night bothered me so much, but it did.

I'm standing outside the bathroom, beneath the blinking blue sign, bright overhead spot, and armadas of bugs swaying to and fro in the still, tropical night air. Occasionally, a sizzle of electricity interrupts the steady hum of the neon sign and the trucks going by. It is the sound of another bug flitting into the electric coils of the mechanical Venus Fly Trap the attendants have mounted above the office door, like a lamp for lost travelers.

I wonder if and when they come out of their office and sweep up the pile of winged corpses gathering on the low cement step outside their door, and, for some reason,

I start walking toward the glowing lantern. What is it about death that makes you want to look at it? What makes you believe you won't blink or turn away? What makes you think that some other death will resemble your own?

For some reason, I'm not sure why, I stop and look back at the car. Either they are asleep in the back or, in Carmelita's case, slouched further down in the front seat of a bright metallic bubble, a toy space ship with big, wide wheels. Whether they're thinking or dreaming, each of them is the sole inhabitant of his or her own planet.

I figure there's no need to get in right then and break the spell that has settled over them, no need to act as if our being together is anything more than an accident from which we can quickly and efficiently extricate ourselves. So I stand here, bathed by the blue light, head swiveling slowly like a periscope, as I look at them, at the trucks and buses disappearing into the gaseous haze, at the bright orange electric coils glowing, like the ribs of a skeleton locked in a furnace, and the bugs getting jolted out of the air. And I tell myself this is as good a time as any to begin learning more about the language of love.

Photo: Peter Muscato

JOHN YAU was born in Lynn, Massachusetts in 1950, and was educated at Bard College (B.A., 1972) and Brooklyn College (M.F.A., 1977). An independent art critic since 1978, he has written for numerous American and European publications, including *Art in America, Art News, Art Press* (France), *Artforum, El Pais* (Spain), *Galeries* (France), *Interview, Tema Celeste* (Italy), and *Vogue,* as well as contributed essays to catalogs and monographs on Anna Bialobroda, Roger Brown, Luis Jimenez, Joan Mitchell, Jackie Winsor, and Martin Wong.

He has taught at Bard College (Milton Avery Graduate School of the Arts), Brooklyn College, Emerson College, Maryland Institute College of Art, Poetry Project (St. Mark's Church), The Writer's Voice (63rd Street "Y"), Pratt Institute, School of Visual Arts, and was a Visiting Professor in the Graduate Creative Writing Department at Brown University (Spring '92), and the Department of Asian American Studies at the University of California, Berkeley (Spring '94).

A recipient of fellowships from the National Endowment for the Arts, the Ingram-Merrill Foundation, and the New York Foundation for the Arts, he was awarded a General Electric Foundation Award and the Lavan Award (Academy of American Poets) in 1988. In 1991, he and Bill Barrette shared the Brendan Gill Award for their collaboration, *Big City Primer: Reading New York at the End of the Twentieth Century.* In 1993, he received the Jerome Shestack Prize from the *American Poetry Review* and was a Visiting Scholar at the Getty Center for the History of Art and the Humanities.

He is currently organizing the Ed Moses retrospective for the Museum of Contemporary Art, Los Angeles; working on a book on the film actress Anna May Wong; and completing a manuscript of poems, *Forbidden Entries.* He lives in Brooklyn.